"But you got amnesia," Aidan interjected with a flat, disbelieving tone. "That's all very convenient."

Violet didn't like his tone. "Are you suggesting that I'm lying about all of this?"

Aidan just shrugged. "It's just a pretty big pill to swallow, that's all."

"I assure you that if all I wanted was to discontinue our..." What was it, exactly? Relationship? Affair? Hookup? "Time together, I would've had no problem just saying so. There's no need to make up a story about amnesia and broken phones just to get out of seeing you again."

"So you did want to see me again." It was a statement, not a question. His subdued grin was unnerving, making her muscles tense and her stomach flip. He seemed to like having that effect on her.

Violet wasn't entirely sure she minded it, either.

* * *

One Unforgettable Weekend is part of the Millionaires of Manhattan series from Andrea Laurence!

D1054420

Dear Reader,

When I was plotting the stories for these Yale sorority sisters, I knew Violet's story would be a different one. For once, I was writing a story with a heroine who had everything and a hero who had nothing. You'd think a billionaire wouldn't have many problems, but Violet has a big one—she doesn't know who the father of her child is! Money can't buy her way out of this situation. An accident has robbed her of a critical week of her life, erasing the memory of her time with Aidan. When he happens to waltz back into her life over a year later, they're both in for some big surprises.

If you enjoy Violet and Aidan's story, tell me by visiting my website at www.andrealaurence.com, liking my fan page on Facebook or following me on Twitter. I'd love to hear from you!

Enjoy,

Andrea

ANDREA LAURENCE

ONE UNFORGETTABLE
WEEKEND

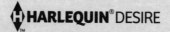

HARLEQUIN® DESIRE

Recycling programs
for this product may
not exist in your area.

ISBN-13: 978-1-335-97156-2

One Unforgettable Weekend

Copyright © 2018 by Andrea Laurence

Printed in U.S.A.

Andrea Laurence is an award-winning author of contemporary romances filled with seduction and sass. She has been a lover of reading and writing stories since she was young. A dedicated West Coast girl transplanted into the Deep South, she is thrilled to share her special blend of sensuality and dry, sarcastic humor with readers.

Books by Andrea Laurence

Harlequin Desire

Brides and Belles

Snowed In with Her Ex
Thirty Days to Win His Wife
One Week with the Best Man
A White Wedding Christmas

Millionaires of Manhattan

What Lies Beneath
More Than He Expected
His Lover's Little Secret
The CEO's Unexpected Child
Little Secrets: Secretly Pregnant
Rags to Riches Baby
One Unforgettable Weekend

Visit her Author Profile page at Harlequin.com, or andrealaurence.com, for more titles.

To Eric—

I was lost when you found me.
Thank you for helping me believe again.

One

"Miss Niarchos will see you now."

Aidan Murphy stood, buttoning his suit coat and smoothing his tie. Wearing a suit again felt a bit surreal after so long without it. At one time, it had been like a second skin to him. Then his world fell apart and the way he lived his life changed forever. A bartender had no need for fancy suits and silk ties. A bartender at Murphy's Irish Pub would be looked at with suspicion by its regular clientele if they walked in wearing this monkey suit.

But today wasn't about Murphy's or the life Aidan lived now or five years ago. Today was about his deceased parents, a deathbed promise and the halfway house he needed to open to honor their memory.

Losing both his parents within a few years of each other had left him things he'd never anticipated—primarily a struggling Irish pub in Manhattan and a huge house in the East Bronx. As a former advertising executive with a degree in marketing, he had enough business savvy to get the bar back up and running, but he had no interest in a house that far away or frankly, that big. He just wasn't ready to part with his childhood home quite so soon after losing them, too.

His parents had bought the place to house the large Irish Catholic family they'd hoped to someday have together and never did. The house itself was paid for, but even if he wanted to sell it, it wouldn't be so easy. The neighborhood was declining and even the rental market there was soft. His mother had known that and urged him to keep it and use the property as a transitional home for alcoholics leaving in-house rehabilitation programs. After dealing with his father's alcoholism, she'd known that a transitional home was the one thing he had always needed after his trips to rehab, but never had, usually sending him right back to the bottle within a few weeks.

That was where the Niarchos Foundation came in, as much as he hated the idea of asking anyone—especially entitled rich people—for help.

Unfortunately Aidan needed money to make his mom's dream a reality. Lots of money. And his personal cash reserves were long gone thanks to his drunken father's poor business practices. So here he was, applying for a grant from the foundation against his better judgment. Somehow that sounded better than begging for money.

He opened the door to the foreboding office and held his breath. It was now or never. Hopefully Miss Niarchos would be susceptible to his charms. He'd found that a smile and a little light flirting could get him what he needed from most ladies. He tried not to abuse his powers, but today, it would make this whole process easier.

Aidan stepped across the threshold into the brightly decorated space and stopped short when his gaze narrowed in on the dark, exotic eyes of the woman who'd vanished from his life well over a year ago. All thoughts of charming the foundation administrator faded as he realized who she was.

Violet.

Violet *Niarchos*, apparently, although full names had never been a topic of conversation during the short time they were together. If they had, perhaps he would've been able to track down his elusive beauty after she disappeared without a trace.

Before Aidan could say hello, he stopped himself. The blank expression on Violet's face was disconcerting. There wasn't a flicker of recognition as she looked at him, like he was just another person coming to her for the support of her foundation, not a man she'd made love to. Obviously the experience had made a bigger impression on him than he had on her.

"Violet?" he asked, just to prove to himself that he was talking to the right woman. He would've sworn it was her, but time could distort the memory. The woman in front of him was more beautiful than even he recalled, and he wouldn't have thought that possible.

"Yes," she replied, standing up and rounding her desk to greet him in a stiff, formal way. She was wearing a lavender silk blouse with a gray pencil skirt, stockings and conservative but attractive gray pumps. There were gray pearls on her ears and a matching strand around her throat. This version of Violet was far more proper and dignified than the one that had stumbled into his bar that night.

"You don't recognize me," he said, stating the obvious. "I'm Aidan. We met at Murphy's Pub about a year and a half ago."

The delicate porcelain of her face suddenly cracked. Her dark, almond-shaped eyes widened and her dark pink lips parted with surprise. It seemed she'd finally pieced together who he was.

"Oh my God," she said, bringing her hands to cover her nose and mouth.

Aidan tried not to outwardly panic as tears started to glitter in her eyes, but inside, he was twisted into knots. In all the nights he'd lain in bed wondering what had happened to her, why she'd never come by the bar, imagining what it would be like to see her again…he'd never anticipated tears. He hadn't done anything to her that would warrant tears.

Had he?

After all, she was the one who walked out of his life, vanishing in the early hours of the morning like a ghost he'd started to think he'd imagined. If he wasn't a teetotaler he'd worry she had been a drunken delusion. She'd felt like one. No real woman could've affected him, touched him, the way Violet had.

If it hadn't been for the taste of her still lingering on his lips and the torn lace panties left behind on his bedroom floor, he might have believed she wasn't real.

"Aidan," she said in a hushed whisper, almost as though she was speaking to someone other than him. A moment later, the tears started spilling onto her cheeks.

He fought the urge to rush over and wrap her delicate frame in his protective embrace. He didn't want to see her cry, especially not at the mere sight of him. But something about the way she eyed Aidan gave him pause. It was probably regret. From the looks of her, Violet was a pretty posh lady. It was likely that she'd forgotten about her two-day tryst with the hot bartender and now that he was standing in her office, she was having to cope with the embarrassment she felt for stooping so low. Otherwise she wouldn't be crying or looking as though she wanted to escape from her pleasant and comfortable office through the nearby window.

"Are you all right?" he asked.

His words seemed to snap her out of her emotional state. She quickly wiped the tears from her cheeks and turned away for a moment to compose herself. "Yes, of course," she said, although he didn't believe her. She turned back, all polite smiles. "I'm sorry. I just…"

She thrust out her hand to shake his. He accepted it, feeling the familiar tingle dance across his skin. Touching her that first night had set his nervous system ablaze and that hadn't changed. The tension in her grip was new, though. It didn't lessen as he touched her. In fact, her hand grew stiffer until she finally pulled away and gestured toward the nearby guest chair.

"Please sit down. We have a lot to discuss."

Aidan took a seat across from her with the massive cherrywood desk separating them. The chair was more comfortable than he expected, the whole office being more an extension of the woman he remembered than the one fidgeting with her paperwork at the moment. It wasn't the typical, sterile business office. There was a seating area with plush chairs and colorful fabrics. The walls had bright pieces of art and photographs of beautiful locations with white buildings against turquoise-blue waters. Where was the woman who decorated this office? The one who strolled into Murphy's Pub looking for something and someone to help her forget her troubles?

"Before we discuss your grant application, I feel like I need to apologize," Violet began. "I'm sure you think quite poorly of me for disappearing. At the moment, I feel awful for doing it."

"I just want to know what happened to you," Aidan replied and that was the truth.

She wasn't the first woman in the world to sneak out of a hookup at dawn, but she never texted or came by the pub again. He practically lived at Murphy's. She could've found him there any time she wanted to, but she hadn't. Their time together had made a huge impact on him, so it had surprised him that she could just walk away from it without a glance back. He'd wanted to look for her a dozen times but had had no way to go about it.

"I was in an accident." Violet frowned at the

desk as she visibly strained to piece together her story. "I guess it must've been right after I left your apartment. My stupid taxi slammed into the back of a bus and I hit my head on the partition. I woke up in the hospital."

Aidan's heart started to sink. He'd never imagined that she hadn't contacted him because she couldn't. He'd been home grumbling into a bowl of cereal and she'd been in the hospital. "Are you okay?"

"Yes," she said with a smile. "I had a good knot on my head, but mostly just bruises. No lasting damage aside from some memory loss. I basically lost the week leading up to the accident. The last thing I remembered when I woke up was leaving my office after a big meeting the week before. I've tried everything over the past few months to recover those memories, but nothing worked. I didn't contact you because I didn't remember you, or the time we spent together, until you walked into my office and said your name just now."

"Are you saying you've got *amnesia*?"

Violet wanted to cringe at the way Aidan said the word. It was the same way whenever someone said it. *Amnesia* sounded like something that only existed in a soap opera, not a real-life medical condition. And yet that was what it was. An entire week of her life had been erased from her brain as though it never happened.

The doctors told her that eventually, the memories would return, but they couldn't predict when or how. She might get little flashes over time or a sense of déjà vu, or it might come back suddenly like a tidal wave washing over her.

It had been the latter. When he looked at her with those big, blue eyes and said his name, it was like the earth had shifted beneath her feet. In an instant, her mind was flooded with images of the two of them together. Naked and sweaty. Laughing. Eating takeout in bed and talking for hours. She fought the urge to blush in embarrassment having such intimate memories about a virtual stranger. But those thoughts were quickly wiped away by the realization of what it all meant for her.

That was what had caused the tears.

She'd spent fifteen months wondering what she'd forgotten when she'd lost that week of her life. Right after the accident, she'd been determined to recover her memories. Eventually she'd put those worries aside when she'd realized she was pregnant. From there on out, her attention turned to her engagement with her longtime boyfriend, Beau Rosso, and planning for the arrival of their first baby together.

Then the baby arrived and the missing week of her life became more important than ever before.

"I know," she said, raising her hand to halt any argument he might have. "It sounds crazy. Until it happened to me, I would've said it was ridiculous, but that's what the doctors told me. I've spent nearly a year and a half trying to get those memories back. But there was nothing, not a flicker of that week of my life, until just now."

Aidan ran his hand through the shaggy ginger curls of his hair and arched his brow. "So, what exactly did you just remember about me?" He awaited her response with a smug curl of his lips.

This time, Violet couldn't prevent the blush the memories brought to her cheeks. She didn't like feeling as though she were at a disadvantage in any situation and knowing he had the ability to ruffle her was unsettling enough. "I, uh," she began, "remember coming into the bar. You worked there?"

At that, he grinned. "Worse. I own it."

Violet nodded, trying not to sigh in relief. She wasn't one to make a habit of having flings with bartenders. She was a shipping heiress to one of the largest family fortunes in Europe and she'd been raised to act accordingly. Her grandfather would roll in his grave if he thought Violet was slumming with a bartender. Then again, she wasn't prone to having flings with bar owners, either, but at least he was a business owner and not a hot guy who paid his rent with a seductive smile and tips.

Violet bit at her lip, trying to sort through all her new memories. She remembered going to the bar, although she didn't know why. It wasn't a place she'd ever visited before. She could recall the exact moment she'd laid eyes on Aidan. Laughing, talking, closing the bar down. "I remember going back to your place."

Her cheeks were burning. There was no way her blush wasn't obvious now. If the red-hot memories weren't enough, the way Aidan looked at her from over the desk would do it. "I think we both know what happened after that," she said.

Aidan nodded slowly. "I've relived that weekend with you in my mind dozens of times, trying to figure out what I did wrong."

Violet pushed aside the stirring images, suppressing the heat that had started circling in her belly. "What do you mean? I may not remember everything yet, but I don't remember you doing anything wrong."

"Well, you left, didn't you? I woke up Sunday morning with a cold stretch of mattress beside me. When did you even leave? I didn't hear a thing."

Violet tried to remember. She had left his apartment early in the morning, but why? Had she had something she'd needed to do? She felt like that was the answer, although she didn't know what it could be. Whatever it was, she'd never made it since she'd ended up in the hospital instead. "I had somewhere I needed to be. I didn't want to wake you up. I was going to call you later."

"But you got amnesia," Aidan interjected with a flat, disbelieving tone.

"Yes. My phone was crushed in the accident, so I lost any new data since my last backup, which probably included your number. Any memories or traces of our time together were erased from my life." Well, most of them. One huge daily reminder remained—she just hadn't realized the significance of it until now.

"That's all very convenient."

Violet didn't like his tone. "Are you suggesting that I'm lying about all of this?"

Aidan just shrugged. "It's just a pretty big pill to swallow, that's all."

"I assure you that if all I wanted was to discontinue our…" What was it, exactly? Relationship? Affair? Hookup? "*Time* together, I would've had no problem just saying so. There's no need to make up a story about amnesia and broken phones just to get out of seeing you again."

"So you did *want* to see me again." It was a statement, not a question. His subdued grin was unnerving, making her muscles tense and her stomach flip. He seemed to like having that effect on her.

Violet wasn't entirely sure she minded it, either. She couldn't remember another man being able to make her stomach flutter with just a glance. Without a touch, with just the memory of a touch, she felt her resolve crumbling beneath her. She wouldn't tell him the truth, but the nights they'd spent together had been the best she'd ever had. He'd mastered her body almost instantly, playing her like a violin until she nearly made herself hoarse screaming out his name. How could she ever have forgotten it?

"I did," she said, swallowing the lump in her throat.

She followed his gaze as it flickered over to her bare left hand. For months, she'd worn Beau's engagement ring. Now the tan line had faded and she'd lost the strange sensation that going without it caused.

"And what about now?"

That was a dangerous question. Spending a weekend with Aidan was one thing, but now… everything had changed. It just wasn't that simple any longer.

"Now isn't relevant," she said, avoiding the answer.

"The hell it isn't!" Aidan stood up from his seat and rounded her desk. He leaned over her, planting his hands on the arms of her chair. He was close without touching her, his warm scent invading her space even as he hovered at the edge of it.

Violet's breath caught in her throat. The large, hulking figure of manhood was so close, tempting her to reach out and close the gap he'd left. The last few months had been scary and lonely. She was tempted to give in to her attraction to him again and let him remind her of everything she'd missed.

"I've spent almost a year and a half wondering what happened to you, Violet. Even when I didn't want to think about you, when I wanted to just move on, the vision of your naked body writhing beneath mine would creep into my head and derail my thoughts." He paused, his gaze flicking over her body then returning to her face. "Now you show back up in my life with this wild story and your big doe eyes and you tell me that your attraction to me isn't relevant?"

How could she explain that things were more complicated than just whether or not she was attracted to him? There were more factors at play, things she needed to tell him, stuff that went beyond her work at the foundation.

Aidan leaned in farther, pausing when their lips were a fraction of an inch apart. Violet's heart was pounding in her chest, her lungs burning with the rapid breaths she was taking. Each one drew his scent into her lungs, reminding her of burying her face in his neck and snuggling into the pillows that smelled like him. He was so close. If she moved, they would be kissing and if she was honest with herself, it took everything she had to stay still.

"Say it," he demanded.

Violet couldn't turn away from his commanding gaze. When he looked at her that way, she'd do anything he wanted. But this wouldn't be just a simple admission of attraction. "Aidan…"

"Say it."

She swallowed hard. "Okay, fine. Yes, I'm still attracted to you. Does that make you happy?"

He narrowed his gaze and eased back from her. "Not really. I've never met a woman who fought her desires so strongly. You don't want to want me at all. Is it because I'm a bartender and not some flashy investment banker like your boyfriend?"

Violet flinched. That wasn't the reason, but it certainly didn't help their situation. She didn't need a man's money—she was a billionaire in her own right—but she had made a habit of dating wealthy men in the past. It made her feel less like a prize to be won, a lottery ticket to change a man's fortune forever. Although they were rarely discussed, there were plenty of male gold-diggers in the world, too.

"No," Violet argued. "It's not about that. And anyway, he's my ex-boyfriend. Listen, there's something we need to talk about." She pressed her hand to his chest, hoping to get some breathing room, but he didn't budge. All she ended up doing was getting a handful of his hard muscles beneath his dress shirt. "Please have a seat so we can talk for a minute."

He didn't respond. He didn't even move. She realized then that his attention had shifted to something over her shoulder.

"Aidan?" Was he even listening to her?

Violet turned and followed Aidan's gaze to the framed photograph on her desk. It was the only picture of Knox she kept in the office, and now she regretted even having this one here. Everyone who saw it asked about the cherubic baby with the bright red curls and big blue eyes. Apparently it had caught his attention as well, but not just because her son was adorable. The similarities were impossible to ignore, a fact that had nearly blown her over when the memories of their time together hit her all at once. At last, the final, crucial puzzle piece had fallen into place.

The panic was evident by his big eyes and slack jaw. He knew what the photo meant. There was no need to do math or conduct a paternity test for him to understand the truth. Finally, he turned back to her and swallowed hard. "Is that your baby?"

She nodded and he stood upright, leaving her personal space and making her suddenly feel cold without him. "Yes. That's Lennox, my son. He's almost six months old."

"Lennox," he repeated, as though he were trying to get used to the sound of the name.

"I call him Knox for short. He's amazing. So smart, so loving. I've truly been blessed as a mother."

Aidan turned back to the photo, the unasked question hanging on his lips.

"And yes," Violet began, with a mix of relief and apprehension climbing up the back of her throat. How long had she worried she would never get to say these words to someone? That she might never know the truth about Knox? Now in the moment, she wasn't even sure she could get the words out. She gripped the arms of her chair to steady herself and looked up into the familiar sky-blue eyes of the near-stranger standing in front of her.

"I'm pretty sure that he's…your son."

Two

"My son?"

Her words were like a swift kick to his gut. Aidan had known—known from the moment he'd laid eyes on the baby in the picture—that it was his, but hearing it aloud carried an impact he didn't expect.

"Yes. I'm sorry this is how you had to find out. Please sit down so we can talk about this."

Aidan reluctantly pulled away and returned to his seat. It was better that he sit, anyway, before his legs failed him and he had no choice. His mind was spinning with thoughts he couldn't grab ahold of. He'd come here to apply for money to start a halfway house and had managed, instead, to get a son. A son named Knox. A son he'd never met before.

The thought made his stomach twist into knots. He'd always wanted a family of his own when the time came. He'd wanted a chance to be a better father than his own had been, to prove that he was better than his alcoholic, waste-of-space dad. He knew that when he decided to get married and start a family, he would dedicate his world to them, because that was the way it should be.

But instead, he'd just found out his son was six months old and he'd missed everything so far. He would remedy that, and soon. He wasn't sure what Violet had in mind, but he would be a father to Knox. He would take him to Yankees games, be there for every T-ball tryout and parent-teacher conference.

"Why didn't you tell me I had a son?" He was surprised at how cold his own voice sounded, but he was choking back a sea of emotions. It was better to show none at all than to let them rush out of him all at once.

Violet's expression twisted in irritation. "You're really asking me that?"

Apparently she was going to stick fast to her amnesia story. He didn't really buy it, but he'd go along with it for now. "So I guess you're saying since you forgot we slept together, you forgot I was the father?"

She slid her chair closer to the desk and folded her neatly manicured hands over the leather and parchment blotter. Her brow furrowed as she seemed to search for her words. "The way you say it sounds so convenient, as though I haven't spent the last six months of my life agonizing over the fact that I had no idea who my baby's father was."

"Who did you think it belonged to for the months before that?"

Her gaze dropped down to her desk, avoiding him. "I thought it was Beau's child—my ex you mentioned before. Since I had no memory of our time together, I had no reason to think otherwise. We got engaged. We planned a wedding and future together. And then the doctor in the delivery room handed him a baby with a full head of curly red hair and the whole room just went into shock."

Aidan tried not to laugh. He could just picture the scene with everyone wondering where this pasty Irish kid had come from. It would be funny if it hadn't meant that he'd missed the birth of his first child in the process. "How'd he take that? Not well I'd imagine."

Violet sighed and looked up at him. "That doesn't matter. What matters is that we're not together anymore and we know he isn't Knox's father. I've got the lab results to prove it."

"What did your parents say?"

She narrowed her gaze at him. "Did we discuss my parents before?"

It seemed as though Violet didn't remember their conversation. That probably had more to do with the tequila than her head injury. She'd been pretty upset when she'd strolled into his bar and demanded a shot with tears in her eyes. He'd listened to her story and made it his mission to make her smile again, never imagining that decision would lead them to this point. To a child.

"Not at length," he explained. "Only that they were pushing you to be with this guy even though he was a grade-A jerk. I can imagine having another man's baby was a disappointment for them after thinking you two were going to get married and they'd get their way."

"Well, yes, but not as much of a disappointment as having an unknown man's baby. They certainly can't have their fancy friends and family finding out the truth. They'd be much happier if I just took Beau back and pretended like Knox belonged to him. I think they're still telling people that Beau is the father and we're just having a rough patch. My mother tried to convince me that we had a recessive pale, redheaded gene in our Greek and Israeli heritage." She shook her head. "I've never met one. They're just grasping at straws."

"I suppose that means they're not going to be

too happy to find out his real father is a broke Irishman who owns a bar."

Violet looked at him with an expression of grave seriousness. He could tell the past year had weighed heavily on her mind. If she was telling the truth about forgetting everything, he imagined it would be difficult. The one week you forget ending up being the most important week of your life.

"I'm not worried about them. In the past few months, I've done a lot of soul-searching and one of the things I've discovered is that I'm no longer concerned with what makes my parents happy. My whole life has been about what makes them happy. Now my focus is on myself and my son, where it should be."

Needing to see it again, Aidan reached out and took the framed portrait from her desk. He ran his finger across the rosy cheeks and bright smile of the child he'd never met. Knox definitely had his coloring, but he had Violet's almond-shaped eyes and full lips. He had her smile, even though his was toothless at the moment. He imagined their son had an infectious giggle the way babies did. He hoped to hear it in person as soon as possible.

"I would've told you," Violet said in a small voice. He looked up from the photo and searched her dark eyes for the truth of her words. "This isn't about other people's opinions or whether or not I wanted you in Knox's life. If I had known, I wouldn't have hesitated to tell you, or to find you again. But I truly didn't remember until now. That's why I cried when it all came back at once. It was an overwhelming sense of relief, finally knowing the truth after all these months."

Aidan sighed and looked back at his son. He wasn't sure if she was telling the truth, but at the moment it didn't really matter. If he wanted to see his child, he'd take her at her word and hope for the best. "So now what?" he asked.

Violet tapped her fingers anxiously at the edge of her desk. "Well, I suppose I should start by calling my attorney. He can get the ball rolling on setting up a paternity test, just to be certain, then we can start working on arrangements for visitation and such."

Only a rich person would start off this process with calling their attorney instead of going for the obvious choice of allowing him to meet his son. Aidan didn't even have an attorney, much less one on retainer who took his calls whenever he needed him.

Of course, Aidan didn't have anywhere near the amount of the money he suspected Violet had. The Niarchos Foundation gave away millions of dollars every year to worthy causes, and that was just a small fraction of the family's fortune. He'd done a little reading about the family when he was looking for places to help with his project. Her grandfather had made a fortune in Greece shipping steel to the United States. When the family came to America, their wealth only grew by leaps and bounds.

Aidan couldn't imagine how many billions of dollars the Niarchos family empire controlled. They probably just started this foundation so the IRS didn't eat them alive. He didn't really like or trust the rich as a rule, but if they were handing out money, he certainly could use some. All he wanted was a small piece to help him kick off his halfway house since every penny he'd saved went into Murphy's.

He never dreamed the daughter and chair of the foundation would be the woman he remembered from all those nights ago. Or that coming here today would put him on a path to meeting the son he never knew about.

"That's all well and good," he said, "and I'm sure it needs to be done, but I was thinking something a little less legally binding to start off with."

"Like what?" Violet asked.

"Like a playdate with my son."

Violet couldn't shake the anxiety that curled up in her belly. It was one thing to agree to Aidan coming over to her apartment so he could meet

Knox; it was another to know he'd arrive any moment.

It had been two days since he'd walked into her office and turned her world upside down. Two days of memories circling in her mind at the most inopportune of times. Memories of the nights she'd spent with Aidan. How he'd held her, how he'd touched her. How he'd made her feel things, both physically and emotionally, that she'd never experienced before.

Losing her memory had at first been an annoyance. When Knox was born, it became an unfortunate complication. Now, knowing how much she'd missed out from her time with Aidan, it had become downright tragic.

How many months had she settled with Beau because she didn't remember how amazing it was with Aidan? All that time, in the back of her mind, she'd had a nagging worry. It wasn't ever something she could put her finger on. Just a feeling that things weren't right. That Beau was the wrong man for her, despite her having no reason to think otherwise.

Now she knew what her subconscious was trying to tell her all this time. Aidan was the man who had been missing from her life. From Knox's life. One look into those sky-blue eyes and she'd nearly been knocked off her feet by the power of that realization. How could she have forgotten that hard, stubble-covered jaw, those skilled lips and those strong hands? Even now, she could easily bring to mind the feel of the coarse, auburn chest hair that spread across his firm pecs. The beat of his heart beneath her palm.

The days and nights they'd spent together had been about more than just sex. It was not at all what she expected, going home with a bartender after last call, but they had really connected. He'd been right about that. Knowing he was back in her life both thrilled and scared her. They'd come together on a level she'd never felt with a man before. It had been as though they'd always known each other after just a few short hours. Like her heart would break if she had to be away from him.

Violet craved that connection again after the tumultuous relationship with Beau ending and the months of emotional upheaval and loneliness that followed. And yet, it frightened her. No matter what happened between them, she hoped that Aidan would be in Knox's life. That was as it should be. But the two of them? Could something that intense maintain itself? Would it eventually consume them?

Even if he was still interested in her—and she wasn't entirely sure that he was—the attraction would eventually die out. They might be drawn to each other just because they'd had their chance taken away. If it ended poorly, she didn't want it to impact his relationship with her son. And if she were honest with herself, she wasn't sure if she could bear the intensity, the passion, and then the crippling grief.

In this situation, it might be better if she kept her distance. Polite. Cordial. Businesslike. After all, they were going to be working together on his grant in addition to raising a child together.

When all the drama had been hashed out, they'd finally sat down to discuss the proposal he'd come for. If the board accepted it, there would be several weeks of working side by side on the project. Her foundation didn't just cut checks, they gave charities the tools they needed to learn how to keep themselves afloat in the future. It was an important key to the success of the Niarchos Foundation, and one that would keep her and Aidan working together no matter what happened between the two of them personally.

Violet heard footsteps coming down the stairs and turned in time to see Tara with Knox in her arms. He was wearing a white onesie with blue and green cartoon dinosaurs on it and little matching blue shorts. It was one of her favorite outfits, a gift from her friend Lucy, whose twins were due any day now. The nanny handed over the baby to his mother and she held him close, breathing in the unexpected scent of his baby soap.

"We had an unscheduled bath just now," Tara

said with a chuckle. "We tried a little applesauce with our breakfast and we got it everywhere. I'm not even sure how much got in our tummy." She reached out and tickled at the infant's belly, making him laugh and squirm in Violet's arms. "He's ready to go, though. All dressed and clean. Do you need me to stay and wrangle him while your company is here?"

Violet bit at her lip, but shook her head no. She'd told the live-in nanny that someone was coming over, but she hadn't said who it was. Good news traveled fast and scandalous news traveled even faster. For now, she wanted to keep Aidan and his relationship with her to herself. "We'll be okay. It's your day off. Enjoy yourself."

Tara smiled and grabbed her jacket from the closet. "Okay. You guys have fun. Text me if you need me."

Tara disappeared down the hallway and Violet breathed a sigh of relief. At least they hadn't run into each other as she left. Aidan was taller than most men, with a solid build that demanded the attention of every woman he passed. Tara would notice him for sure. And with that fiery red hair and those icy blue eyes, there was no way anyone would look at Aidan and not know exactly who he was.

That wasn't to say that Violet didn't trust Tara. She loved her. Any doubts or concerns she'd had about hiring a nanny had gone out the window when Tara interviewed for the position. Violet had basically been raised by nannies. Her parents were always on the move, touring the world, securing business deals back in Greece and a dozen other countries. Their private jet had more miles on it than most jumbo airliners. But that meant that Violet had grown up alone with no one but her hired caretakers.

They had all been lovely women. Not horribly strict or harsh, but they hadn't been suitable replacements for her parents, either. When Knox came along, she knew she needed help doing this all on her own. She had a job and since it was a family business, she could take him in with her if she had to, but he really needed someone during the day. Tara had been the perfect someone. A helping hand, but not a substitute like her own had been.

But the situation with Aidan was a precarious one. She wasn't ready to trust anyone with it yet, even Tara. She hadn't even told her best friends from college—Emma, Lucy and Harper—about Aidan's arrival. That would come in time, she was sure, but on her own terms, not because of out-of-control gossip.

Violet looked down at her son. He was chewing intently on his fist with slobber running down his arms. He might be clean, but her little monkey was never perfect for long. She walked over to the Pack 'n Play that was set up in her home office and grabbed a clean burp cloth to wipe away the drool. "We don't want you drooling all over Daddy first thing, now, do we?"

Knox just grinned, shoving his fist back into his mouth the moment she released it. The books said he was teething and any moment now, the first few would start to break through. She anticipated quite a few long nights with a cranky baby in her future.

The phone rang. Violet eyed the number, knowing it should be the bellman calling about her guest. A "Mr. Murphy" was waiting for her in the lobby. She told them to send him up and tried to prepare herself for his arrival.

It seemed to take ten minutes for the elevator to crawl the five stories to her apartment. She wasn't in the penthouse, but she was fairly high up in the building with her apartment taking up the west side of the fifth and sixth floors. It gave her nice treetop views of Park Avenue. She'd had the apartment—a graduation present from her parents— since she'd graduated from Yale and moved back to Manhattan. It almost made up for the fact that they hadn't been able to attend her commencement in New Haven. They'd been stuck in Istanbul. She wasn't surprised. That had been their MO her whole life—lavish gifts in exchange for the emotional and physical distance between them.

Soon, though, Violet wanted to make a change. The apartment was spacious when Violet was alone, but a little too small for her, Knox and Tara. Baby things seemed to fill every corner. She wanted more room and to be closer to a park where Knox could run around. Central Park was a little too chaotic for her to keep up with him there. She got a feeling that this little monkey would be on the move the minute he learned to walk.

The doorbell rang. Violet took a deep breath to prepare herself. It should be easy. Today wasn't about her. It was about Aidan and his son. But that didn't mean it wouldn't be a heart-wrenching moment for everyone involved.

Violet walked to the front door and opened it, stepping back far enough to allow Aidan a full view of her standing there with Knox in her arms. "Hello, Aidan. Come in."

She might as well not have spoken because the instant his eyes connected to his son, the whole world faded away for a moment. He didn't move. He didn't even appear to breathe. Aidan was frozen to the spot as he studied his child for the first time.

Knox, however, was oblivious to their visitor. He'd become fascinated with the scalloped edge of Violet's collar, pinching it between his clumsy, chubby fingers.

She turned a bit so Aidan had a better view, then tugged Knox's hand from her shirt. "Lennox, we have a visitor. Can you say hi?" He couldn't, of course, but Aidan had finally caught his attention. Knox's big eyes locked in on him and he grinned wide.

"It's amazing how much you two look alike," Violet chattered nervously in the silence. "I bet in your baby pictures you couldn't tell you two apart."

Aidan just shook his head, apparently ignoring everything but Knox. "A part of me didn't really believe all this until now, but it's true. He's my son."

Violet winced and glanced over his shoulder into the hall beyond him. The neighbor she shared a vestibule with was incredibly nosey. "He is. Come in and you two can spend some quality bonding time together."

He finally took a few steps into the apartment, allowing Violet to shut the door. He studied the child in her arms like an exhibit at an art gallery, trying to absorb and process every detail from a distance.

Violet looked down and noticed he had a gift bag in his hand. He'd need to put that down to hold Knox, which she was certain would come next if he could work up the nerve. He seemed both anxious and terrified about the prospect. "Why don't you follow me into the living room where you can set your things down and get more comfortable?"

She turned, and he followed her until the hall opened up to a large contemporary space filled with light from the nearly floor-to-ceiling windows along two sides of her corner unit. In the center of the room, she'd put a grouping of comfortable white couches, the only splash of color being some blue throw pillows in the mostly white and gray space.

"Have you been around many babies before?" she asked. She wasn't sure what his level of skill or comfort was with an infant. He could've raised his siblings or have another child she didn't know about, unlike herself who had almost never even held a baby before Emma's daughter, Georgette, arrived. For some reason, the thought of Aidan having another child made her jealous on Knox's behalf.

"No, not really," he said at last. "I was an only child. I don't have any kids of my own—I mean, I don't have any *other* kids. He's my first. Basically, I'm clueless."

Violet smiled. It seemed like a big admission for a man like him. She could tell that coming to the foundation for a grant had bothered him. His initial posture as he'd come through her office door had been defensive. He read like the kind of man who was used to being able to handle anything thrown his way without assistance from anyone. The fact that he'd come to her anyway because his project was important was something she appreciated. Knox was obviously important to him as well, or he likely wouldn't have admitted his inexperience there, either.

"You'll do fine. I didn't know much when I started either. He's not a small and fragile newborn anymore, so you won't have trouble. He's a sturdy boy, at the top of his percentile of weight and height for his age."

At that, Aidan beamed with paternal pride. "I've always been pretty solid. I would've made a decent football player if I'd wanted to, but baseball was always my sport." He held up the bag to show it to Violet before setting it on the coffee table. "That's actually some Yankees outfits for him to wear and baby's first baseball mitt. Now that I'm involved, I've got to make sure you're raising him right."

Violet chuckled. "We're not Mets fans in my family, so no worries there. The foundation actually has a box suite at the new Yankees stadium if you'd like to take him to a game." She shifted Knox in her arms until he was facing out. "Here," she said. "Why don't you go ahead and hold him? You'll get over your nerves faster that way."

She watched as all the muscles in his body tensed. Memories of touching each and every inch of them flashed through her mind as they flexed beneath his skin. She missed touching a man—the hard muscles, coarse hair and heated skin against her own. So different and yet so comforting. Now wasn't the time to reminisce about what she'd lost. She pushed the thoughts aside and focused on easing their son into his arms for the first time.

Aidan appeared nervous for a moment, but Knox snuggled comfortably against his chest and the tension lessened in him. He cradled him easily, instinctively bouncing a bit on the balls of his feet. "Hey there, little guy," he said.

Violet took a step back to give them some space and shield him from the tears that were forming in her eyes. She watched through blurry vision as Knox put his hand against Aidan's cheek and giggled at the feel of his stubble. He hadn't been around very many men, but he seemed to instantly take to Aidan. Perhaps he knew his father instinctually. Or perhaps Knox was just as drawn to Aidan as his mother was.

Watching the two together was such a touching moment for Violet. After everything she'd experienced over the past year, she'd begun to wonder if she'd ever get to witness a moment like this…if Knox would ever get to know the protective embrace of his real father. She'd been racked with guilt after Knox was born. Guilt for misleading Beau, although unintentionally. Guilt for not being able to remember something as important as who her baby's father was. Guilt of knowing he might grow up never knowing his father, and his father never knowing he had a son, just because a taxi driver got impatient and wiped the memories from her mind.

Then Aidan had walked into her office and the opportunity suddenly appeared to put everything to rights. They'd all been given a chance to start again and do things the way they should've been done to begin with. Now she couldn't understand why she'd been so anxious about Aidan's visit. She couldn't be more grateful to witness this touching moment between father and son. She'd cherish this memory forever.

It was special. *Perfect.*

And then Knox puked applesauce down the front of Aidan's polo shirt.

Three

If you'd told Aidan six months ago that he'd be half-naked in Violet's apartment today, he would've laughed. Then again, back then he hadn't known about his new son or factored in how far the boy could projectile vomit applesauce.

"I just put your shirt in the dryer, so you should be able to wear it home," Violet said as she came back into the room with Knox on her hip.

After the applesauce incident, Aidan and Knox had played while Violet cleaned up and threw their clothes in the washer. She'd quickly changed the baby into a little outfit with a train embroidered on the chest.

"I don't really have anything in the house that would fit you." Violet's gaze ran over his bare chest, then shifted quickly to the art on the wall over his shoulder. "I'm sorry about the mess. Having an infant has been hard on my drive for perfection."

"It's my fault," Aidan admitted. "I should know better than to bounce a baby if I'm not sure how long it's been since he's eaten last."

"I suppose you'll always remember the first time you held your son, now," she said with a chuckle.

"How could I forget? Even without the spit up it's a pretty momentous event."

Aidan noted that his words brought a shadow across Violet's face, stealing the light humor from her words. Her gaze dropped to the floor in contemplation. Suddenly she seemed sad, although he wasn't sure if it was because he'd missed out on the first few months of his son's life, or because he'd finally caught up with her. His unexpected arrival had to be a complication to her life.

Aidan took the moment to study Violet. He hadn't really had the chance to do that in a long time. When she'd shared his bed, he'd lain beside her and tried to memorize every line and curve of her face. The delicate arch of her dark eyebrows, the thick fringe of her lashes against her cheeks as she slept…

Today she looked different than before. Like that night at Murphy's, she was still dressed flawlessly from head to toe with styled hair and a full face of makeup. This time, she had on impeccably tailored plum slacks and a silk blouse with a collar embroidered with tiny flowers. But something wasn't quite right. She looked less peaceful than she'd been sleeping in his arms all those months ago. More at the mercy of life's stresses, with lines around the edges of her eyes and etched into her forehead. Despite having been pregnant, she seemed thinner than before the baby. Almost hollow. Drained. The last year and a half had clearly been hard on Violet.

Although you wouldn't know it to look at him, it had been hard on Aidan, too. Losing his father three years ago had turned his life upside down, but it hadn't been unexpected. He'd bounced back. Murphy's was doing good business again and although he wasn't a hotshot advertising executive anymore, he'd been happy with where he was in life.

Then his mother got sick.

Owning their own business, they'd never had medical insurance growing up and health care reform had done little to help where she was concerned. She'd had the cheapest catastrophic plan, all she could afford, but it hadn't been enough once she got sick. The best treatments, the latest and greatest advancements in Europe, were well out of their reach. The big pharmaceutical industries were charging thousands of dollars for a single dose of medication that could've worked wonders for his mother. They had to recoup what they spent on research and development, they argued. But that argument couldn't keep his mother from succumbing to her illness.

Aidan had never felt more helpless in his life as he had watching her waste away in a state-run hospital. His father had killed himself with alcohol, but his mother hadn't done anything but be too poor to afford the treatment that could have saved her.

Before she passed, his mother did leave him with one task he could control—the halfway house. It had been her idea, one she couldn't see through to the end. But Aidan could, and he would do it with the help of Violet's foundation. Life had come full circle in a strange way.

Violet turned to look at Knox as he yawned. "I think it's naptime for this little guy. Would you like to help me put him down?"

He looked up at Violet and Knox and smiled. "Sure," he said and accepted the baby into his arms.

The clean, babbling ginger baby went contentedly to Aidan. He hadn't been around many babies but those he had tried to hold had never been too happy about it. He was thankful his son felt differently. He liked holding his son just as much as Knox liked being held. He smelled like baby shampoo and talc, a combination Aidan wasn't used to but found soothing somehow. Knox curled contentedly against Aidan's bare chest and shoved his fist into his mouth.

"Be careful he doesn't get ahold of that chest hair," Violet warned. "Come this way and I'll show you his nursery."

Looking anxiously at the chest hair he wanted to keep, Aidan fell in step behind Violet. He followed her upstairs and down a hallway to a door that opened up to a spacious and beautiful room for a baby. It was decorated in a gray-and-white chevron pattern with pops of bright yellow and dark blue. There were elephants on the curtains and a large stuffed elephant in the corner of the room. He couldn't imagine a more perfect nursery.

Violet stopped in front of the large white crib with elephants on the bedding. Aidan watched as she turned the switch on the mobile overhead, making the matching menagerie of elephants in different colors and sizes dance around in a circle to soft music.

"You can just lay him down there," she said. "He'll be out cold in minutes."

Aidan eased his son into the crib, knowing he needed his nap and yet not ready to let go just yet. He had to remind himself that he would see Knox again.

The baby squirmed for a moment, then reached out to snatch a pacifier from Violet. He sucked contentedly as his eyes fluttered closed.

"Told you," she said. "He loves his naps."

"Like father, like son," Aidan replied with a smile.

Violet grinned. "Let's go."

They crept quietly out of the nursery, and Violet shut the door behind him. Instead of heading into the living room again, however, Violet crossed the hall to the door opposite Knox's. When she opened it, Aidan was taken aback to find it was her bedroom.

Why were they going into her bedroom?

She went inside without hesitation or so much as giving him a second glance. He stayed in the hallway, not quite sure what the right course of action was. When they were at her office, before he'd known about Knox, he'd pressed Violet about her attraction to him. He didn't really need to ask. Aidan could tell by the flush of her cheeks and the way she nervously chewed at her bottom lip that she still wanted him. He just needed her to say it out loud so she would admit it to herself.

Violet had finally broken down and confessed that she still wanted him, but that conversation had gotten sidetracked not long after and they'd never returned to the topic. Was this her way of circling back to where they'd left off?

He didn't know Violet well. At all, really. But he couldn't believe for a second that the beautiful, rich perfectionist he'd come to know was leading him into her room to seduce him while their son napped across the hall. He'd like it if she did, of course, but he doubted it would happen.

"Aidan, you can come in," she said from the far side of her bedroom. She was standing in front of a large oak dresser with a mirror. Between them was a queen-size bed with a plush floral comforter, an upholstered headboard and about a dozen different fancy pillows. Apparently rich people liked to spend their money on pillows.

He gripped the door frame and held his ground. He wasn't entirely sure that he could refrain from touching her once he set foot into her bedroom. It was too personal somehow, like she was opening up to him. He could already smell her familiar and enticing scent as it lingered there. It called to him. Another touch, another taste, another aspect of his missing fantasy woman was all he'd craved these past lonely months.

"I don't know if that's a very good idea."

Violet frowned at him, her gaze traveling to his bare chest again and staying there a moment too long. When her eyes met his, he could tell she'd been admiring his physique and thinking the kind of thoughts that could get them both into trouble. The blush had returned to her cheeks as she licked her dry lips. He understood how she felt. He'd been having enough of those thoughts about her since he'd arrived and she'd been fully dressed the whole time.

"I'm grabbing something out of my dresser. I'm not trying to seduce you, Aidan."

He crossed his arms over his chest in a thoughtful posture. He wasn't so certain of that. "Are you sure? You were just looking at me like I was a tall, cool glass of water you were dying to drink. And to be honest, I'm pretty thirsty myself."

"I may have been looking, but that's all I was doing." She turned back to the dresser and pulled out something folded. "I can't help but look when you're half-naked like that. Here. It's the largest, manliest shirt I own and I need you to put it on, please."

Violet tossed the shirt to Aidan. He caught the wad of fabric and shook it out to investigate what she'd offered him. If this was the largest, manliest thing she had, he couldn't imagine what the rest was like—lace and bows and glitter? For one thing, the shirt was too small. He had broad shoulders and a wide chest that demanded an XL top even when his waistline was on the narrow side. The top was a medium, and a woman's medium at that. It was also a purply sort of color. Its only redeeming attribute was the black logo on the front for a local rock band that he'd heard play a time or two.

"This is too small."

"Please put it on."

"I'm going to tear it."

"It doesn't matter. I just need you to wear it until your shirt dries. It's that or a pink silk robe. Your choice, but you've got to wear something."

There was a pleading in her eyes that he couldn't ignore. She was desperate not to want him. There were lots of reasons she could feel that way. Perhaps she didn't want to complicate the issue with sharing custody of their son. Maybe she was in a relationship with someone else. Or she could be embarrassed that she had little self-control when it came to her attraction to a lowly barkeep. That was one reason to fight your feelings. Not a good one, but still a reason.

With a shrug, he attempted to pull the T-shirt over his head. It wasn't the easiest thing he'd ever done, but after some tugging and grunting, he was able to pull it down to cover most of his stomach. "Okay, it's on."

She didn't respond right away. He looked up at Violet and found the stunned expression on her face unexpected. Despite the fact that he was wearing a ridiculously small purple shirt that belonged on a woman, she looked at him as though she could eat him with a spoon. She was actually gripping the footboard of her bed with white-knuckled intensity.

"What?" he said, looking down at himself. It was easy to see the issue. The shirt was tight. Painted-on tight. Every twitch of his muscles, every line of his six-pack abs, was magnified by the clingy top she'd forced him to put on. Her plan had backfired spectacularly.

"Oh, dear. We should've gone with the robe." She sighed, shaking her head. "Just take it off. It didn't help."

"The pants, too?" Aidan asked with a sly grin.

Violet swallowed hard before shaking her head. "Uh, no. Just the shirt."

For now at least, he thought with a wry smile as he tugged the purple fabric over his shoulders.

"You've been quiet this week, Violet," Harper noted over her traditional girls' night glass of dry merlot.

"Is Knox teething yet?" Emma asked. "When Georgie started teething, she hardly slept a wink at night, so neither did I. I was a zombie for weeks and that was with a nanny helping during the day."

"Is that what I have to look forward to?" Lucy asked with concern lining her brow.

"Times two," Harper pointed out with a smug grin. She was the only single one in the group without a baby on the way, so she was well-rested, thin and living a fabulous life from all outward appearances. "So expect it to be exponentially worse than Emma and Violet have had it."

"I appreciate you pointing that out, dear sister-in-law," Lucy grumbled into her glass of Perrier and lemon instead of her usual sweet rosé. She was thirty-five weeks pregnant with Harper's niece and nephew. She and Harper's brother, Oliver, had gotten married a few months ago and had been anxiously awaiting the arrival of the twins.

"That's what I'm here for," Harper quipped. "So seriously, what's going on with you, Vi?"

Violet had much preferred her friends continue with the banter so she didn't have to answer Harper's pointed question. Unfortunately, she could tell her friend wasn't going to let it go. She knew that girls' night would be the night she'd have to come clean to them. They could sniff out a secret like a bloodhound.

Knowing it was time to spill the truth to her best friends, she took a deep breath and began. "Knox *is* starting to teethe, but that isn't it. Something else has happened."

"Oh, really?" Emma said, leaning in curiously to hear the latest news. "Do tell."

"Beau hasn't started sniffing around again, has he?" Lucy asked in a worried tone.

It wasn't the first time she'd heard that, and for

good reason. Violet's ex-boyfriend had tried to reconcile with her a few times in the six months since Knox was born. He'd actually been all too happy to continue their engagement and marry knowing Knox wasn't his son. He insisted that he loved her and he didn't care about Knox's parentage. It had been Violet who'd demanded the paternity test, and Violet who had returned the ring and ended things when the results came back the way her gut had anticipated them to. Beau hadn't been any happier about the breakup than her parents had been, but she knew she had to do it.

"No, thankfully I haven't heard from Beau in several weeks. This is actually good news. I had a major breakthrough with my amnesia."

"You remembered something?" Lucy asked with wide brown eyes.

Violet nodded. "Not everything," she admitted. "But the most important parts, I think."

"Knox's father?" Emma asked with a breathy voice.

"Yes."

Violet's three best friends in the world whooped with excitement, drawing stares from others around the restaurant. They quickly started a rapid fire of questions, hardly leaving Violet time to answer.

"Just relax for a minute and I'll tell you everything," Violet said, holding up her hand to slow their words. She shook her head and steeled her own nerves with a large sip of her chardonnay. "Last Monday, a man came into the foundation."

"Did he have red hair?" Lucy asked.

"Let her tell it," Harper complained.

"I am letting her tell it," Lucy snapped.

"Yes, he had red hair," Violet interjected into their argument. "And blue eyes just like Knox, but even then I didn't recognize him at first. He knew me, though. Apparently he thought I had run out on him the morning of my accident and he didn't know how to find me."

"When did you get your memories back?" Emma prompted.

"When he said his name. I didn't have the slightest idea who he was and then all of a sudden, it was like a bucket of memories was dumped on my head. I remembered nearly every second of the two amazing days we spent together. And at that point, there was no doubt in my mind that Aidan was Knox's father."

"Ohmigosh," Lucy gasped and clutched her huge belly. "This is so exciting I just might go into labor."

"Please don't!" Harper said with panicked eyes. "The twins need to stay in there as long as they can. If you go into labor on girls' night, my brother will blame me. I don't want to have to hear him complain."

"That has to be a relief for you," Emma said, ignoring the others and reaching out to clasp Violet's hand. "Now you finally know who your baby's father is. I only went a couple months when I first got pregnant before I tracked down Jonah. I can't imagine how you've dealt with the uncertainty for all these months."

"I didn't really have a choice," Violet said with a dismissive shrug. The last six months had been hard, no doubt, but there wasn't much she could do about it when her brain wouldn't unveil its secrets.

"What's his name?" Harper asked. "I have a friend at FlynnSoft that can run a background check on him if you'd like me to ask."

"No, that won't be necessary, I don't think. I know plenty about him already from his grant application. His name is Aidan Murphy." It felt nice to finally know that answer when she was asked. Even when she remembered him she didn't know his last name. They hadn't exchanged much personal information, including last names, when they spent time together before. She didn't know it until she looked over his paperwork.

"So did you tell him about Knox?" Lucy asked.

Violet nodded and reached out to grab some spinach dip from the bowl in the middle of the table. She was suddenly more interested in eating than talking but at this rate, the dip would be cold before she got any if she didn't just dig in.

"He figured it out before I got the chance when he saw the baby picture on my desk. That's when I came clean…"

The girls pestered her for the next hour, asking her to go over every detail of her reunion with Aidan and his first visit with Knox. They gave her a break long enough for everyone to order dinner, but the questions continued as they ate their entrées and ordered another round of drinks.

"Wow," Harper said as Violet wrapped up her tale. "Did you remember anything else about that week? The time with Aidan was just the last two days before your accident, right? You don't remember what happened before that?"

"No, not yet." That had bothered Violet, but she'd been too busy with the situation with Aidan to give it much thought. Something had sent her to Murphy's Pub looking to drown her sorrows in liquor. She wished she knew what it was. At the same time, one major breakthrough at once was more than enough. It would come to her eventually, she hoped.

"You don't seem very happy," Emma noted. "I thought you would be more excited about all this. I mean, you didn't even tell us about it and it's been almost a week since it happened. What are you leaving out?"

Violet was hoping they wouldn't pick up on that, but of course they would. "Maybe I'm just overwhelmed by the whole thing. It's a lot to take in. Now I have to start the process of sharing Knox with his father when he's been all mine since the day he was born."

Harper shook her head. "That's not it. There's something else. Have you told your parents about Aidan yet?"

"Heavens no!" Violet exclaimed. "I want Aidan and I to work things out in terms of raising Knox and get it settled with our attorneys before we bring my parents into the situation. You know how they are. Besides, they're in Dubai right now. Or Qatar. I forget which."

"I get the feeling it wouldn't matter if they were at the next table. What are you leaving out? What's wrong with Aidan? Is he weird? Annoying? A Communist?"

"There's nothing wrong with him," Violet argued. "He's just not what I was expecting. Not the kind of guy I would usually date."

"The kind of guy you usually date is an asshole. So that's a good thing, right?" Harper wasn't holding back tonight.

"Beau wasn't an asshole," Violet argued. "We were good on paper. It just didn't work as well in real life. Aidan is…"

"Poor?" Lucy interjected.

Violet turned to her friend and wished that she could say she was wrong because it sounded so snobby that way. Lucy had grown up with nothing, and until she inherited a fortune from her employer—Harper's great-aunt—she probably had less than Aidan.

"Poor isn't exactly how I'd phrase it," she argued. "He owns his own business, but he's in a different social circle than I usually date in. I know that sounds horrible, but you all know why I do that! My family is famous and any guy with a computer can Google my net worth without much trouble."

"Poor billionaire Violet," Harper said with a smile that undercut her sarcasm. "So what kind of business does he own?"

"A bar. An Irish pub to be exact."

"That's why you haven't told your parents, and took your time telling us," Harper said with an accusing tone. "You had an affair with some sexy bartender!"

Four

It had been a couple days since girls' night, but their words still echoed in Violet's head. That she was keeping secrets about Aidan. That she hadn't told her parents or her friends because she was embarrassed about slumming with a bartender. That maybe, deep down, it was true.

No. It wasn't true, and yet their words haunted her. She knew Aidan was more than just a bartender. Along with her hotter memories had come some of their pillow talk. She knew he was a smart, capable, caring man. One who would be a good father for Knox.

But that still didn't mean she was going to tell her parents about him.

It wasn't about Aidan, not really. It was her parents who were the problem. They jet-setted around the world, ignoring her most of the year. When she did see them, they were filled with criticisms and loaded down with gifts. The gifts soothed their conscience and also doubled as bribes. While she was still lying in the recovery room, her father had offered her a luxury yacht if she'd agree to marry Beau and tell the world he was Knox's father.

She'd turned that offer down.

It was probably one of the first times in her life she'd put her foot down with her parents. They hadn't quite known how to take her answer. So they'd given her a diamond watch as a push present, opened a trust fund for Knox and got back on a plane to somewhere else.

Her parents loved her. Violet knew that on a practical level. But they weren't the hands-on, demonstrative parents she'd always wanted. She wanted that for Knox and she felt like Aidan would provide the warm father figure he needed.

She just knew her parents wouldn't see the good in Aidan. Only his "flaws," the way they focused on hers. She'd already done enough to Aidan, albeit not deliberately. If she'd had her memories she would've told him about Knox the moment she realized she was pregnant. He didn't deserve the kind of casual abuse her parents would heap on him—comparing him to Beau at every chance,

criticizing his work, his family, his upbringing…
No good would come from that. For now, it was
easier to let them think her memories were still
lost in some dark corner of her mind.

She had spoken with her attorney, however, and
wanted to talk to Aidan about his recommenda-
tions going forward. Violet decided to stop into
Murphy's before it opened. He texted that he would
leave the door unlocked so she could pop in whenever she could.

When she arrived outside the bar, she felt the
intense sensation of déjà vu. This was the place
where her life had changed forever, even if she
hadn't known it until recently. As she pushed open
the heavy door to step inside, the familiar scents
and sounds of the bar surrounded her. Behind the
bar was Aidan, polishing glasses from the dish-
washer and putting them away in their respective
homes.

"Welcome to Murphy's Pub." He greeted her
with a warm smile that made her belly clench.

That smile was probably what had lured her
to him the night they met. He had almost a mag-
netic pull on her. She wanted to be close to him.
Even now, although she wrestled with it, she felt
the draw. Of course she wanted him as a father
for her son. And she still wanted him for herself
if her jacked-up pulse and aching breasts were any
indication. But did they have long-term potential?

She wasn't sure about that. They were from disparate worlds. Different cultures, different religions, different neighborhoods. He might never be comfortable rubbing elbows with the ultra-wealthy families the Niarchoses associated with. It had been easy to ignore those differences for a weekend when there was no promise of anything more, but for a lifetime? It would eventually be an issue.

"Where is Knox?" Aidan asked when she came through the door with nothing but her designer handbag.

"He's with Tara." Violet couldn't very well bring her six-month-old son to a bar, even if it was to see his father. She set her purse on the newly cleaned bar top and climbed onto one of the worn stools that lined it.

"Who's Tara?"

"She's the nanny."

Aidan got a funny look on his face. It was a mix of surprise, irritation and a complete loss of vocabulary. She wasn't sure why he was confused by something that simple. He should've expected that she had someone to help her with the baby. Violet was a single, working mother. Someone had to keep Knox during the day. Eventually, he would go to a prestigious preschool, but until then, she had to choose between a nanny and day care. The nanny route won in the end.

"What?" she asked at last. "There's something on your mind, say it."

Aidan sighed and slumped onto the bar stool beside her. "What do you really know about this Tara? Did you do a background check on her? Get references from other families?" he asked.

Violet snorted and shook her head. Did he really think she would leave her child with just some random person off the street? "'Yes' to all of that. I actually know more about her than I know about you. She checks out on every level and she's amazing, so you can take the protective dad thing down a notch."

He shrugged off her concerns. "I can't help it. I'm new at this, but it's amazing how quickly the parental panic sets in."

"I know. When they took him from my arms to do his checkup at the hospital, I started to worry. By the time they gave him back to me, I was on the verge of tears. I had never loved anyone as much as I loved that little boy the moment I laid eyes on him."

Violet noticed a sad look in Aidan's eyes before he shook it off and pasted his bright smile back on. She wished she could give him back the six months he'd lost. Or at least kiss him until the sadness faded away.

"So whatcha drinking?" he asked, changing the subject.

"Do you have anything sweet?"

"I have a Magner's Irish Hard Cider on tap."

"I'll take that." She picked up a cardboard coaster and started spinning it absently between her fingers while he moved down the bar to pour her drink.

Aidan set the glass on a napkin in front of her. "So you mentioned when you called earlier that you spoke with your attorney. What did he have to say about our little situation?" he asked.

"He's going ahead with a draft custody agreement for us to meet and redline. His assistant will also call you with a time and place to go for the paternity testing. The lab already has Knox's profile from his first testing with Beau. Basically, we'll start from there."

"Okay, but I'll need to know how much I'll owe in monthly child support and things like that, too."

The mention of child support brought Violet's fidgeting to a standstill. "I didn't tell my attorney to ask for child support."

Aidan stopped and looked at her with his ginger brow furrowed in confusion. "Why not? I'm willing to do the right thing and help support my son."

Violet felt her stomach tighten with anxiety. She hated talking about money, especially her own money. It was one thing to talk about the family wealth in abstract or the foundation, but her personal finances always seemed to open up a door to angst. People never looked at her the same way when they knew how much she was worth. She liked the way Aidan looked at her that night after Murphy's closed. His blue eyes had reflected pure desire and nothing more. Even now, she could catch the light of appreciation there as he admired her appearance from across the room. She didn't want that to change. But she couldn't take his money just to end the awkward conversation.

"I don't need it, Aidan," she said at last. "With you trying to start the halfway house and keep the bar running, you can put that money to good use elsewhere. At the very least, save it for things to do when you and Knox are together."

"I have to," he insisted with a stern set of his square, stubbled jaw. "I'm his father. I don't want people to say I didn't step up when the time came."

"And I'm telling you that I can't take a dime from you. I mean it." Violet crossed her arms over her chest in defiance. She doubted it made her appear more adamant, but she'd try it anyway. Male pride could be so frustrating sometimes. That was one thing about Beau that was easier to handle. He was happy to let her pay for things when she wanted to.

Maybe too happy in retrospect.

Aidan looked around the bar and held out his arms. "Listen, you're well-off, Violet. I can tell by the apartment bigger than my bar and the nanny and everything else. But I—"

"I'm not just well-off," she interrupted, feeling the frustration building in her neck and shoulders and pulsating a familiar pain down her arms. She took a sip of cider, hoping it would relax her and dull the pain.

Although she had a really nice apartment and most everything she needed or wanted, she tried to live a more modest lifestyle by Manhattan standards. Her parents' collection of homes was so lavish she was embarrassed to take anyone to visit them. As a teenager in prep school, she'd never hosted a single sleepover. Not that her parents were ever home to oversee one. Her schoolmates didn't need to see the gold-plated furniture and the marble statues of Greek gods in the foyer. It was an over-the-top display of wealth that made her uncomfortable.

"Aidan, I'm one of the wealthiest women in the country," Violet said, finally spitting out the words she'd been holding in. "We're talking billions. With a *B*. I'm sorry to be so blunt about it, but I need you to understand that I'm not just being nice when I say that I don't need any of your money."

"She's a frickin' billionaire?"

Aidan winced as one of his regulars, Stanley, said the *B* word a little louder than he would've liked. "Why don't you yell it again, Stan? I don't think the whole bar heard you the first time."

"Sorry," Stan said, taking a big swig of his dark brown pint of Guinness. "I thought you were bragging. I know I'd be happy to be involved with a sexy billionaire. I'd shout it from the rooftops."

"You'd shout it from the rooftops if you were involved with *any* woman."

Stan chuckled and took another drink. "Probably so. But what's so wrong with a rich girl?"

"Nothing. And everything." Aidan didn't like to admit it aloud, but he didn't really care for rich people. Give him blue collar…give him salt of the earth people who worked with their hands and were willing to give you the shirt off their backs… He'd rubbed elbows with all types and the working class were the kind of people he preferred to associate with in both his personal and private life.

There were never ulterior motives to their friendship. They weren't out to make a buck off you or use your shoulders to climb higher up the social ladder. Most of them knew they were never going to be upper class, much less rich, and they were okay with that. Aidan had aimed high, trying to better his situation for his and his mother's sake, and he'd done well. Working at one of Madison Avenue's biggest and most prestigious advertising agencies had come with lots of cash and plenty of perks.

But he was happier here behind the bar at Murphy's Pub. Aidan had had a taste of upper class and it was far more sour than he'd expected it to be. Here, if something tasted bad, he just changed out the keg and the problem was solved.

"This is about what happened with you and fancy pants Iris, isn't it?"

Aidan winced at the mention of his ex-fiancée's name. "I paid you fifty bucks to never say her name again."

Stan rubbed his stubbly chin thoughtfully. "You said you would. Never did, as I recall. So I'll say it again. That nasty breakup with Iris must've made you bitter."

Bitter? Aidan thought over Stan's choice of words and eventually shrugged it off. "Maybe so. Wouldn't you be bitter if your supposedly loving fiancée left you for your wealthier, more successful boss?"

"He wasn't your boss," Stan pointed out. "You'd quit the agency by then to come work at the pub. I remember her coming in here to break it off."

"Technicality. What's important is that she decided—within weeks of my father's death, I might add—that marrying a bar owner wasn't good enough for her. If I wasn't going to be a hot shot advertising exec with a chance at making partner at the agency, she wasn't interested."

"That was pretty cold. But what makes you

think this new woman you're involved with would do the same thing?"

"I don't." Aidan shook his head and wiped down the worn wood countertop of Murphy's Pub. Most of the day-to-day tasks of running Murphy's were the kind he could go through almost robotically without concentrating too hard. Unfortunately today, that meant his mind was free to run through his earlier conversation with Violet again and again. "It's just a general distrust of the wealthy. The rich get richer, the poor get poorer, and the rich are happy to keep it that way. Anyway, I'm not *involved* with Violet. I was. We have a child together thanks to some tequila and a three percent failure rate on condoms. I don't think she's interested in, uh…"

"Banging the bartender on the regular?"

"Nice choice of words there, Stan. But yes. Our fling was one thing. An actual relationship is totally different."

"Just because it's different doesn't mean she's disinterested."

"She didn't exactly run out to find me when she realized she was pregnant. Would you if you were in her shoes? I'm just a bartender barely keeping afloat, Stan. She's probably embarrassed to tell people about me."

"I thought she hit her head or something."

"That's what she says."

"You don't believe her?"

Aidan sighed and leaned his elbows on the countertop. "I don't know. It seems awfully fantastical. The far simpler answer is that she wanted to forget she ever met me and when put on the spot, she came up with that story so she didn't look like the bad guy."

"Or she really did have an accident and forget. She's been very accommodating since you two ran into each other, hasn't she?"

She had. That was part of the problem. The Violet he knew didn't seem like the kind of woman who would make up a story like that. She'd seemed genuinely relieved to know his name and connect the dots of her past. But did that Violet from all those months ago have anything in common with the high-class lady who had his baby? It was hard to associate those two parts of her personality.

"Let me ask you this, then," Stan said when Aidan didn't respond to his question. "You say she wouldn't want to date you. But what about you? Are you interested in a relationship with her?"

Aidan's jaw clenched tightly as he thought over his response. Easily, the answer came that he wanted her. How could he not want her? She was the most beautiful, sensual creature to ever waltz into his life. But the Violet he wanted was the one who had stumbled into his bar all those months ago. Was billionaire socialite Violet going to be as uninhibited and free? Knowing more about her and who she really was by the light of day had changed things for him.

As Stan had mentioned, Aidan didn't exactly have the greatest impression of rich people, and it wasn't just because of Iris and that toad Trevor. No, he'd been burned more than once by people with more money than moral fiber. Violet may not fit into that category, but he didn't know for sure. As she'd pointed out earlier that afternoon, they didn't really know much about each other. It wasn't long ago that he didn't know her last name or where she lived or worked. What he did know—what he had burned into his brain—was every curve of her body, the taste of her skin and the soft sounds she made just seconds before her orgasm broke.

"It's too early to say." Aidan answered the question at last. "It's complicated."

Out of the corner of his eye, he caught the unmistakable gesture of the two men drinking in the far corner. They wanted another round. Aidan moved away from Stan and poured two pints of beer. Then he carried them over to the table and bussed their empty glasses.

"All relationships are complicated," Stan pointed out when he returned. "What makes this more complicated than usual?"

"Aside from her being ridiculously wealthy? How about that if something were to happen between us now it has the potential to complicate our coparenting arrangement?"

"Coparenting?" Stan said with an expression of distaste. "What's that, raising a kid together?"

"Yeah. That's what they call it now."

"When I was young enough to get a woman in trouble, they called it *marriage*."

Marriage? He supposed that some people would think that was the answer. Aidan was actually lucky his devout Irish Catholic parents were both dead and buried or the news of their illegitimate grandson might have killed them.

"Yeah, well, the topic of marriage hasn't even come up and I'm not in the least bit surprised. Why would she want to marry me, Stan? She doesn't need me to raise our son. She has a fortune at her disposal. The biggest Manhattan apartment I've ever set foot in. A live-in nanny. Me showing up in her life is mostly a complication for her, I'm sure. She's letting me be involved in Knox's life to be nice. There's nothing I can offer her or my son."

"That's not true," Stan said in as comforting a tone as he could muster. The older, burly, rough construction worker was hardly the comforting type. "You're his father. At least you're pretty sure you are. Once the tests come back and you're certain, there's nothing that will ever change that and no one else that should take that place in his life. You don't need money or a fancy job to be

there for your son. Just be a dad. That's important. More important than bleeding your check-
ing account dry trying to pay for the kid's fancy
private schools. She can handle that. You stick to
what you're good at."

"And what's that?" Aidan asked. "I used to be
good at getting people to buy things they didn't
need. In high school, I was a decent baseball
pitcher. I can pour a perfect beer. None of those
skills will help me where Knox is concerned."

"Just be the best dad you know how to be," Stan
grumbled. "Is that so hard?"

"I don't know. Do I know how to be a good
dad?" Aidan asked.

Stan looked at him with a narrowed gaze. "You
didn't have the best example in your father," he admitted. He'd been a patron of Murphy's Pub long
before Aidan took over and had been good friends
with Patrick Murphy, his father. "But I've known
you since you were a kid and you've grown into
a good man, Aidan. You gave up your career to
take over this place after your dad died. You took
care of your mother while she was sick, God rest
her soul. You know how to be a good dad because
you're a good person. I'm certain of it."

Aidan thought over his regular customer's
words carefully before he nodded. "You're right,"
he said at last. "Being there is more than some

dads do, rich or poor. I'm just not sure if that's enough for a kid like him."

"A kid like what?"

"A rich kid. I can't buy him a sports car or send him to some Ivy League school like other dads can. But I want to play catch with him and take him to his first Yankees game. I want to teach him what he needs to know to be a strong, honorable man in this world, so when he grows up with a fortune at his disposal, he doesn't abuse his powers. I also want him to have a normal childhood."

"What's normal?"

"Having a trust fund opened the day you're born isn't normal. Neither are boarding schools, live-in nannies and being captain of the polo team." Aidan shook his head. "No matter what I say or do, my son is going to be a rich kid. That's a given. All I can do is try to keep him levelheaded so he isn't a spoiled, obnoxious rich kid."

"Good luck with that," Stan said, taking the last sip out of his pint glass. He shuffled off his stool and tugged his coat back on.

Aidan chuckled at his regular and went to close out his tab. "Thanks."

Five

The sound of the phone ringing—again—was enough to set Violet's teeth on edge.

That morning, she'd stepped out into her kitchen and found herself ankle deep in cold, murky water. Understandably, her day had gone downhill from there. Hours of phone calls, troops of repairmen and insurance company paperwork had left her slightly less damp, temporarily homeless and extremely irritable. So when the doorman rang to let her know she had another guest, she wasn't exactly receptive to the news. But it was Aidan, so she said to send him up anyway.

She waited in the foyer as Aidan stepped out

of the elevator and stopped. Her front door was standing wide-open with a huge industrial fan blowing in on the wood floors. His eyes were wide with surprise as he ran his hands through his long strands of auburn hair.

"What the hell happened here?" he asked as he took a giant step over the fan into her apartment.

Violet sighed and pointed to the disaster area she once called a kitchen. "Apparently one of the pipes from the upstairs bathroom corroded and finally burst in the night. It took out my kitchen ceiling and filled most of the apartment with several inches of water. This is one of the joys of living in a pre-war building, I guess. I never expected to wake up to a mess like this."

Aidan looked around with a grim set to his jaw. "This is going to take a while to fix. The wood floors will have to be replaced. They're already warping. Some of the floor and ceiling supports, too. The insulation soaks up the water inside the walls, so that might have to get ripped out and replaced along with all the drywall that got wet. Maybe even the cabinetry. It's a big job, for sure."

"Do you know much about construction?" Violet asked.

He shrugged. "Not really, but I've done some jobs here and there. Dad's bar flooded during Superstorm Sandy and I had to help with some of that. I'm going to be doing most of the renovation of my mother's house when we get the money. It will help me stretch the dollars further. I know it takes time, though. Did the repairmen give you a timeline?"

"No, but I've basically given them a week to get it back to functional. If they do a good job I might pay them later to renovate the kitchen. I was thinking about doing that at some point anyway."

"A week isn't very long for all that work."

"Well, with the amount of money I'm willing to pay to fix this, they can figure out how to get it done. I can't stand to stay in a hotel for longer than a week at a time, and that was before Knox came along. As it is, it's going to be a tight squeeze with Tara, the baby and me. Even a suite at the Plaza is going to feel claustrophobic after too long with all of Knox's things."

"The Plaza?" Aidan said with a strange expression twisting his face. "Are you serious?"

"Yes," Violet said, not entirely sure why he thought it was an odd choice. It was just down the street and convenient. "I already made the reservations. We can't stay in the apartment when it's a construction zone. Tara is packing up her and Knox's things right now."

"You don't have family you can stay with? What about your parents?"

Violet stifled a laugh, covering her mouth with her hand and softly shaking her head. While it did seem like a logical option, there was no way she was packing up and going home unless she had no other choice. Even with her parents out of the country, she'd suddenly be fourteen again and they'd be in her business, having the house-keeper spy on her and report back. And they'd be in Aidan's business if he came around the apart-ment, as well.

"No, thank you. I'd rather stay in a hotel than do that. I've told you how they are."

His blue eyes searched around the room for an answer, although she doubted he'd find it among the warped wood and soggy insulation tiles. "What about staying with me, then?"

Violet stopped and it was her turn to frown. "With you? Don't be ridiculous."

"It's not ridiculous," Aidan said. "You've been to my place before. It's not the Plaza by any stretch, but I've got two roomy bedrooms and a full kitchen, which you won't have at the Plaza. I'm at work most of the time, so you'd have the place to yourself. It's just for a week and it would give me more time with Knox."

Violet tried not to be offended that he wasn't interested in more time with her, although his offer did leave her with a few important questions. "That's a sweet offer, but two bedrooms," she re-peated, "for three adults and one baby." Where did he think everyone would end up sleeping in this scenario of his?

"Tara and Knox can share the guest room. It has a double bed and his Pack 'n Play will fit in there just fine. You can sleep in my room. And I…" Aidan's deep voice drifted off as his bright blue eyes met hers from beneath their heavy ginger brows.

Her belly tightened when he looked at her that way, the possibilities dangling in the air between them. Sharing an apartment, a bedroom, a bed… It didn't matter if it was for a week, a day or an hour, Violet wasn't sure she had the willpower to keep away from Aidan. Images of him standing shirtless in her bedroom still haunted her at night. It had taken everything she had not to run her fingers through the auburn curls on his chest and drag her nails across the hard muscles of his stomach.

"…I will sleep on the couch."

Or maybe she wouldn't have to use willpower.

Even then, she couldn't accept his offer. Staying at the Plaza was hardly an imposition. They would have housekeeping and room service and they would survive. "No, really, Aidan. I'm not going to impose on your life. The hotel is fine. They're sending over a shuttle van to pick us and our things up in an hour."

Aidan grabbed her cell phone from the kitchen counter and handed it to her. "Call and cancel it."

"What? Why?" Violet snatched the phone out of his hand but didn't have any intention of calling anyone. Instead, she shoved it into the back pocket of her jeans.

"Because I'm not letting you and my son live in a hotel when I can do something about it."

"Let me?" Violet couldn't help the edge in her voice. She wasn't the kind of person who asked permission from anyone. At one time, her parents had watched and critiqued her every step, even from halfway around the world. As she grew up, she decided that anyone else could mind their own business. She learned early on that there were plenty of people in the world—men especially— who would be happy to control her and her money. But she was not a prize to be won. Violet had to grow a backbone or she might as well give her fortune away.

"Who are you to *let me* do anything? I am a grown woman—a single mother at that—who makes her own decisions."

Aidan's eyes widened as he realized his mistake and held up his hands to buffer the blowback. "That's not what I meant. I know you make your own decisions, probably better ones than I do. I just want to do something nice for you, okay? You've been great helping me with the foundation grant and working through the custody situation with Knox. There isn't much I can do for you or

Knox. I'm sure the Plaza will be great—far superior to anything I can offer you. But I'm asking you to consider staying with me instead. Let me do this for you."

Violet sighed and crossed her arms over her chest. The pleading expression on Aidan's face was hard for her to resist. She knew it was tough to be involved with her in any capacity. The few friends she'd kept around and the men she'd dated over the years had told her as much. Buying her presents seemed impossible. What do you buy the person who can quite literally buy almost anything they want? And helping her? With what? She could pay for all the help she might ever need.

True kindness though… That wasn't something you could put a price on. She could tell Aidan wanted to do this for her. Not to impress her or keep an eye on her, but because he wanted to be nice. From what she remembered of his place, it was a nice apartment in Hell's Kitchen. It wasn't all the way downtown or worse, far off in Jersey or something. She remembered him telling her that the place was the only thing left from his old life, although she couldn't remember what he was referring to now.

"It would be nice to have a full kitchen for Knox," she admitted. The Plaza only offered a mini bar and she doubted they had baby food and warmed formula on the room service menu.

"Okay. We can try it. But if it's too tight of quarters or it's just not working out for some reason, the three of us will head to the Plaza."

"Absolutely. And I'll gladly help you move there if I'm wrong." The wide grin on Aidan's face was the best thank-you she could've gotten. "But I think it's going to be great."

Violet wasn't so sure, but she knew it would be a better alternative than living in the disaster area of her apartment for the next few days. There was no way Knox could nap or Violet could think with all the work going on. "Thank you, Aidan. This is a very kind offer. I hope we don't make you regret it. Knox is cutting his bottom teeth with a vengeance."

"No worries. I've missed so much that I'll happily endure teething to spend time with him. And you," he added with a pointed look into her eyes before he quickly shifted attention to his watch. "Uh, listen, I'm going to run home and clean up so everything is ready when you get there." He scribbled the address onto a slip of paper in his pocket and handed it to her with a brass key. "I've got to head to Murphy's about two, so if you're not there before I leave, you'll need this."

Violet accepted the address and the key, holding the cool metal tightly in her hand. "Thank you, Aidan."

He nodded and slipped back out the door, stepping wide over the fan drying the floors. Once he was gone, Violet looked down at the key in her hand. The ache in her stomach made her think she'd made the wrong decision staying with him. The ache in her core when he'd looked at her that way made her certain of it. If she didn't want a relationship with Aidan, she needed to tread very carefully. But what was done was done.

It was only a week, right?

With a sigh of resignation, she went up the stairs to the nursery and let Tara know about their sudden change of plans.

Aidan quietly unlocked the front door of his apartment and slipped inside, not sure of what he might find when he got there. He'd had to leave for work in the midst of their settling in. He'd called home to check in a few times throughout the evening and Violet insisted everything was fine, but he wasn't so sure. There was an edge of anxiety in her voice. Then again, she'd had a long and frustrating day that started with wet ankles and ended in another man's apartment.

The apartment was dark and quiet. It looked almost as though nothing had changed today aside from little touches—bottles in the drain tray by the sink, the stroller sitting in the foyer and Violet curled up on his couch with a book.

The only light in the room was shining down

on her, highlighting her form like she was an angel sitting there. Her long, dark hair was twisted up into a messy knot on top of her head and she was wearing a pair of navy silk pajamas as she read. He wasn't sure if she'd ever looked as beautiful as she did then, fresh faced and relaxed.

When she finally looked up at him and smiled with a divinely serene look on her face, Aidan had to brace his hand on the back of a chair to steady himself. "Hi," he said, as ineloquently as he could manage.

"Hi." Violet put a bookmark between the pages and closed her book.

It was then that he noticed it was a historical romance novel—the kind where the man on the cover was wearing nothing more than a kilt and a broadsword while he gripped a woman in his arms. The golden script on the front said something about The Highlander's Bride. Prize? The Highlander's Pride? He wasn't sure. Either way it was not what he would've thought would be in Violet's "to be read" pile. She'd always struck him as the book club type. Interesting.

"I didn't expect you to still be up." He hadn't closed tonight, but when he did, it was after four in the morning when he got home.

"I've got a lot on my mind," she said in a low voice as she stood up from the couch and walked over to him. "How was work?"

"Same as any night," he said. He didn't want to bore Violet with the realities of drunks he dealt with every evening. "Did you guys get settled in here okay? Does everything suit you so far?"

"Everything has been great. It's a single man's apartment for sure, but we're doing fine. We spent the afternoon doing a little childproofing, but nothing too major. Knox isn't on the move yet."

For that, Aidan was thankful. He wasn't that great with childproof locks. Grown-man-proof locks was more like it.

"I also did some work from home," Violet continued. "When I checked my email this morning, I got a message from the foundation chairman. They met this morning and you'll be happy to know that the board approved your grant proposal for the full amount you requested."

Aidan's heart nearly stopped in his chest. The full amount? Approved? He almost didn't believe it. "Are you serious?"

Violet nodded and grinned. Before he could stop himself, he reached out and scooped her into his arms. She squealed with surprise as he lifted her off the ground and spun her around the living room.

"We got the money!" he shouted, growing dizzy with excitement and the circles they were spinning around his blue shag area rug.

"Aidan!" she scolded in a harsh whisper, but he

hardly heard her. It wasn't until the words "wake up the baby" made it to his ears that he realized it was three in the morning and not the best time for celebrations.

He slowly lowered her back to the ground, torturing himself by letting each inch of her body rub along his own until she was back on her bare feet. His pulse started pounding furiously in his throat, making it hard for him to draw in a much-needed breath of cool air. He also had a hard time letting go of Violet now that he had her in his arms again.

Aidan hadn't intended to touch her, hadn't let himself do more than shake hands with Violet since they'd reunited, and for good reason. Sweeping her into his arms had been a reflex and now, a part of him regretted it. Now that he'd done it, it would be ten times more painful to let her go. If he could let her go. The part of him that didn't regret touching her wanted to continue. He forced himself to disentangle from around her, but his hands stayed firmly in place at her waist. He willed himself to release her, but he couldn't do it.

What he did notice was that Violet wasn't pulling away, either.

They stood close together, both of them struggling to catch their breaths from the sudden rush of excitement surging through them. He was relieved to know he wasn't the only one affected by this. Violet was physically flustered with a rosy pink highlighting her cheeks.

"I'm sorry," Aidan whispered as he dropped his forehead to rest against hers. "I just was in desperate need of some good news and you gave it to me."

Violet's gaze shifted toward the guest room as she held silent and still for a moment listening. "I don't think we woke him up," she said at last with a heavy sigh of relief. Her eyes met his with a mischievous twinkle lighting their dark brown depths. "Not for your lack of trying." She smacked him playfully on the chest.

Aidan feigned pain, but all he felt was the pleasurable surge that went through his body as she touched him again. What he noticed was that she didn't move her hand away after she hit him. They both stood there in his living room—his hands encircling her narrow waist, her palm caressing his chest. He wished he could whip his shirt over his head so she could run her fingers though his chest hair. He loved it when she did that. Aidan could still remember the feel of her fingernails grazing across his skin. Just the thought of it combined with their bodies so close was enough to build the pulsating arousal in him.

Aidan tried to wish it away. This whole physical interaction between them tonight was a fluke. He hadn't even kissed Violet since that day all

those months ago. Them sharing his apartment for
the week wouldn't change anything between them.

Or would it?

"Aidan?" Violet's soft voice called to him, both
a question and a plea.

He knew how to answer it. Aidan leaned in
to her and brought his lips to hers. The moment
they touched, it was like a wormhole opened up
and sucked them in. Suddenly they were together
again, fifteen months ago, with none of the com-
plications or repercussions in their way. It was just
Aidan and Violet giving in to the pleasure of one
another's embrace.

Violet didn't flinch or pull away. In fact, her
mouth was soft and welcoming, opening to him
and letting her tongue gently caress his. She
melted against him, the soft curves of her body
molding to his hard edges.

Aidan groaned softly against her lips, hoping
he wasn't too loud. He wasn't about to let this
moment be interrupted by babies or nannies or
anything else. He'd fantasized about and waited
for the opportunity to hold her again. For fifteen
months, he'd wondered if she would remain a
memory and nothing more.

And now, her hands were roaming across his
chest, and his tongue was grazing her teeth.

"Aidan?" she whispered against his lips a second time.

This time he paused, still cupping her flesh by the handful through her blue silk pajamas. "Yes?" he asked as he silently prayed for her not to put the brakes on this encounter. He wasn't ready to give up this moment quite yet, even if it was a bad idea. He would deal with that in the morning.

"Take me to your room," she said instead.

His heart leaped with joy in his chest and he didn't hesitate for a moment. Instead, he took her by the hand and led her through the dark apartment to his bedroom. Thankfully, his room and the guest room were separated by the kitchen, giving them a little privacy.

He tugged her inside and swung the door closed. With that barrier up between them and the outside world, it was as if a dam had broken. Whatever willpower Aidan had was washed away in an instant and all he could do, all he could think about, was getting a naked Violet beneath him.

She seemed to feel the same way. They both tugged at each other's clothes, her silk and his cotton being tossed unceremoniously onto the floor. The moment new skin was exposed, they'd stop to caress and taste the newfound territory before moving on.

The next thing he knew they were both completely naked and falling back onto his bed. The queen-size mattress had a good bit of give, breaking their fall and sending them bouncing several inches back into the air. Between laughter and kisses, they settled into the bed, pushing aside pillows and blankets until they were fully aligned and unfettered.

This first time, Aidan knew, would be about letting the pressure off. Months of denial, days of wanting and not touching, had built up between them. Romance, foreplay…it was all out the window in the quest to satiate the need inside them both.

"Condom," Violet whispered between panting breaths as Aidan knelt between her thighs and sucked hard at her breast. He teased at her opening, pressing into her moist flesh. She was right. He knew if he didn't stop now to get it, he would do something they both regretted.

Not that doing the right thing last time had made a bit of difference. They'd used plenty of condoms without fail, and yet they had a son together anyway. This time, as he reached for the bedside drawer, he was comforted to see he'd purchased a different brand than before. Just to be safe.

Aidan slipped the latex over the length of his desire and returned his lips to hers. His hands caressed her breasts, her rib cage, then slid down her side to her hips, where his fingertips pressed into the ample flesh of her rear. He held her perfectly still as he slowly moved forward. When he was fully buried in her welcoming warmth, he let out a ragged breath of relief.

He'd thought he'd never experience this divine feeling with Violet again and yet against all odds, she was in his bed. He hadn't expected it or planned for it when he'd walked in the front door that night, and yet here he was, reliving his fantasy with her.

Violet drew her legs up and wrapped them around his hips, pulling him deeper. Aidan let out a groan, smothering it against her lips.

"Give me everything you've got," Violet whispered with a twinkle of mischief in her dark eyes.

Aidan didn't hesitate to fill her request. He wrapped his arms around her, holding her tight and still against him as he began thrusting hard into her. Again and again he pounded into her body to the chorus of Violet's muffled cries. She buried her face in his neck to stifle the sounds, alternating between moans and sharp nips against his throat.

It was all too much for him to take—overstimulation to the max. As much as he wanted to hold on, to make this moment last all night, he couldn't maintain this for much longer. She was too beautiful, it felt too good and his senses were on overload. He was counting down to his climax, but before he could give into it, he felt Violet start to squirm and buck her hips hard against him. He responded in kind, thrusting harder and faster until he felt her start to tense and finally come undone beneath him.

At last she broke into a silent scream as she clawed at his back. Her head went back and her body bowed up against his, then began to shudder and writhe with her pleasurable spasms. Her inner muscles clamped down on Aidan and before he could stop himself, he found his own release inside of her.

Then, just as quickly as the moment had come upon him, it was over. After hovering over her, breathing hard in his recovery, Aidan rolled onto his back and pulled away. Snuggling was nice, but leaking condoms were not. He needed to deal with that. And then…he realized he wasn't quite sure what to do after that point.

Their constant live wire of sexual tension had propelled them forward faster than their burgeoning relationship called for. After taking that leap to intimacy, where did that leave them? Were they dating now? Was it a onetime thing? Would she want him to stay in the bed with her or would the awkwardness fill the space that had once held passion? Aidan wanted to avoid an embarrassing situation between them at all costs. They would be spending the next week together in close quarters no matter what happened tonight.

Finally he got up and went to the bathroom to

clean up. That was step one. He'd worry about the rest after that. When he returned to the bedroom, he grabbed a pillow and a pair of jogging shorts to take with him to the sofa. That was easier than asking if she wanted him to go.

"Where are you going?" Violet asked, still naked and strewn temptingly across his mattress.

Aidan shrugged. "To sleep on the couch."

Violet arched a brow at him and chuckled as she pushed up onto her elbows. "Do you really think that's a necessary precaution after everything that just happened between us?"

That was a good question. A part of him was relieved that she didn't expect him to leave. But he had promised her this room and that he would sleep on the couch when they discussed staying here. He didn't intend to break his word, but with her lying naked in his bed, tangled in his sheets with swollen lips and tousled hair, he didn't really want to walk away, either.

To be honest, he wanted her again. Slowly. A second chance to take his time and indulge his every sense in her body. By the light of morning, everything might change and he needed to make the most of this while he could. "I don't know," he answered.

"You get back into this bed right now!" she demanded at his hesitation. Then she smiled with the wicked glint returning to her eyes. "I'm not done with you yet."

This time he was all too happy to comply.

Six

Violet was having a hard time focusing today.

Aidan was in the office going over plans and paperwork for his grant and she couldn't concentrate on the task at hand. Not with him looking at her so seductively and smelling like her favorite tasty treat—him. All she could think about was burying her face in his throat, tasting his skin and drawing his distinctly male scent into her lungs.

Practically, she knew she should regret last night, but she had a hard time making herself feel that way. It didn't feel like a mistake to give into her desires for Aidan. It felt like the most natural thing in the world. Their time together in the past had been so amazing it was difficult to deny herself something she knew they both wanted. They'd wanted it enough to succumb to temptation four times that night before the sun came up. Every movement of her body brought an achy reminder of their time together.

Then again, their situation was more complicated than it had been the first time they came together. She tried not to let herself go down the rabbit hole of wondering what it would mean if they continued to see each other, and how they would handle other people finding out about them. Violet had no concerns about Aidan's background, job or financial situation, but she knew others would feel differently. Like her parents. Their friends. She wanted to protect Aidan from the uglier parts of her social circles—the ones that would judge and whisper about him. They did it about everyone for one reason or another, but he would be fresh meat for the gossipmongers. He didn't deserve to be dragged through the mud just for being with Violet.

But really, there was no "them," so her worries were premature. Yes, they shared a child and for a short period of time, an apartment, but sleeping together one night wasn't a guarantee of a relationship by any means.

And for now, she was okay with that. Relationships were hard work, if the one with Beau was anything to compare to, and they both had enough on their plate right now. Giving in to their attraction and having fun while they were together was almost therapeutic—a stress reliever better than a glass of wine or a run on the treadmill. Could the physical turn into more? There was certainly that possibility, but that didn't make her want him any less.

Right now, she couldn't imagine anything that would be a turnoff where Aidan was concerned. To be honest, if she knew her assistant, Betsy, might leave early today, she'd lock her office door and let him take her across her desk. All he'd have to do was push up her skirt…

Violet glanced up from the paperwork she'd been blankly starting at and found Aidan looking at her with a sly grin plastered across his face. "What?" she asked, as she felt a blush warm her cheeks. Did he know what she'd been imagining just now? It felt like she'd been caught red-handed.

"You're not listening to me at all. You're a thousand miles away."

She bit at her lip sheepishly and shook her head. "No, I wasn't listening to you. I'm sorry. I got lost in my thoughts for a minute. Repeat what you said, please."

"I hope they were dirty thoughts," he teased.

If he only knew…

Aidan shuffled the paperwork and pointed his

finger at one of the sections he'd highlighted in yellow. "But seriously, I was asking about this part in the paperwork that talks about helping my new organization build its own donor base. How will we do that?"

Violet took a deep breath and launched back into work mode. She was more comfortable there than in thoughts about her involvement with Aidan. "While we provide funds to you, we also provide connections to a network of other charitably minded people and organizations. Typically, we will do some kind of event to help you draw donor support, raise some additional funds and connect you with people that may want to be involved with your organization in the long-term. Our hope is that the money we give you is seed money to get the charity off the ground and that eventually, you can support yourselves."

"What kind of event are you talking about?"

Violet picked up a couple invitations from past occasions they'd put together. She kept a file of them to use as examples. "Sometimes we do a walk or fun run. Themed parties or galas are always well attended. There's been a few carnivals. A concert. You get the idea. Galas are probably our most successful events. The return on investment is pretty good and you don't have the major outlay for bringing in a celebrity or something. Rich people like to dress up and mingle, and doing it for charity makes them feel good. With any event, you're really just looking for something to get some publicity for your charity."

Aidan flipped through the cards she handed him with a thoughtful look on his face. "I never imagined doing something on this scale."

"You've got to if you're going to get word out about— By the way, what are you going to be calling it? I never quite know what to refer to your halfway house as when I'm speaking about it."

He sat back in his chair and thought for a moment. "For a while I was playing around with Stepping Stones or something like that, but eventually I let that go and decided I kind of liked Molly's House. That was my mother's name and it was her house, after all. It was her dream to help people like my dad recover from their addictions since she couldn't save him."

"Your father was an alcoholic?"

Aidan nodded. "It's what killed him in the end. And I can't help but think that the years of stress on my mother contributed to her illness, too."

Violet tried not to think about how rough it must have been on Aidan to lose both his dad and his mother, and so close together. He was older when it happened, but it still seemed to define him in some ways. He dedicated his life to running that bar and making it successful again. He fought to open this facility in his mother's memory when it would've been so much easier to just sell the house and move on.

She appreciated how much he cared about the people in his life. He would be a great father for Knox, and a wonderful husband to whatever lucky lady snagged him. Somehow, she didn't think that would be her, even if she wanted it to be.

"That's a great name." Violet reached for one of the forms and filled out the line for the organization title. She needed to focus on the event, not on who might be lucky enough to be with Aidan someday. "Having a name can also help with the event planning," she continued. "See what flows well, like the Friday Suppers Fun Run. We did that race for a local soup kitchen."

Aidan looked down at the stack of invitations she'd handed him before dropping them onto the table. "You know, I think a party would be the thing to do. You said they turn a nice profit and that's what we need. Maybe a Midnight Ball for Molly's House?"

That wasn't bad. A shame it wasn't closer to the New Year. "How about a Masquerade for Molly's House? We could do a black-tie party and encourage everyone to wear Mardi Gras or Venetian-style masks. That's a little different from the usual party and yet I think a lot of people will have fun with it."

He nodded. "I like that. A Masquerade for Molly's House. I think Mom would've liked that, too, especially everyone wearing masks. She always made a big deal out of making my costumes for Halloween each year."

"Great. With that kind of setup, Molly's House will earn the profits on every ticket sold after we recoup costs for renting the venue, entertainment, refreshments and such. The most valuable part of the event is collecting the names and contact information of all the attendees for your future fundraisers, but the cash is great, too. We can do some additional things like a raffle to raise more money. Perhaps we can get a local company to donate something valuable, like a diamond necklace or a car to raffle off."

"An actual car?" Aidan asked with wide, surprised eyes.

"I've done it before. We gave away a sporty little BMW one year. The dealer basically sold us the car below his cost for the advertising they would get. We charged twenty-five dollars for each raffle ticket, and it did so well, we paid for the car and made a tidy profit on top of that. It was something different that the attendees enjoyed. It doesn't have to be a car, of course. We could come up with something that's meaningful to you and your organization."

Aidan looked at her for a moment as his brow furrowed with thought, then he ran his fingers through the strands of his copper hair. "What about a trip?"

That wasn't a bad idea. They hadn't done that before. "What kind of trip?"

"My mother always wanted to go to Ireland. It had been her dream to visit the village her family came from and tour all the sites. After my father died, she even made plans to go there with a group of ladies from the church, but she got sick and had to cancel before they went. She was diagnosed with pancreatic cancer, which is so aggressive and difficult to treat. She fought so hard and only lasted about eight months from her first oncologist's appointment. I would love it if we could give away a trip for two to Ireland. You wanted something meaningful, and that would fit the bill more than a BMW."

Violet smiled. That was a perfect suggestion and one she wouldn't have ever thought of on her own. "That's an amazing idea. I'll get my assistant, Betsy, to call my travel agent and see if they could get us a good deal on an all-expenses-paid trip for two. I know a few people at an airline. Perhaps we could get first-class airfare or a week at a hotel donated. Make it really nice, so the donors will be excited to buy raffle tickets."

This was really coming together and she was excited by its potential. Violet reached out and took Aidan's hand as it rested on her table. The sudden movement seemed to startle them both since they hadn't touched since this morning, but neither pulled away. Instead, he looked at her and smiled. The warmth of his skin chased away the chill she always felt in the air-conditioning of summertime, and the heat in his gaze made her core feel like it was molten inside. She didn't know how she could possibly want him again so soon after last night, but she did.

While she was hopeful to have her apartment back in one piece soon, staying with Aidan wasn't bad at all. The Plaza was nicely decorated with all the amenities of a five-star hotel, but the master bedroom didn't come with a sexy ginger to keep her warm at night the way his apartment did.

A soft tap at the door caused their hands to repel from each other as they both turned to see who was there. She saw it was her long-time assistant as she poked her head inside.

"Yes, Betsy?"

"I'm sorry to interrupt. I just wanted you to know that Mr. Randall is here for your three-o'clock appointment."

"Thank you." Violet looked down at her Rolex and realized the time with Aidan had flown by faster than she'd expected it to. "Well, at least we got a great start on planning. With your first check, you can start renovations on the house. In the meantime, I'll get more of the gala information together for you to look over later this week."

"Okay. This all sounds really great, Violet. There's only one problem I can foresee."

Violet straightened up in her seat. She didn't like the sound of that. She worked really hard with the foundation to ensure that every event went flawlessly. "What's that?"

"You're planning a black-tie affair and I don't own a tuxedo," Aidan said with an apologetic smile.

Even at the peak of his advertising career, Aidan hadn't owned an expensive suit. He had some that were nice—nicer than anything else he'd owned in his whole life—but they weren't even close to the kind of clothes in the windows that Violet was perusing.

Ralph Lauren, Tom Ford, Giorgio Armani…all he could see were dollar signs running through his brain. He shouldn't have said anything to Violet, he knew now. He'd set her on a mission. He should've just shown up at the ball in a black rented penguin suit and no one would've known or cared where it came from.

But Violet apparently cared.

"I think an Armani or Tom Ford is the right style for you," she said aloud as they looked into the windows at the store on Fifth Avenue. "They're trending toward a slimmer fit this season. It will require less tailoring."

Aidan followed her inside the Armani boutique with a dismayed expression on his face. He could hardly afford the food served inside at the restaurant, much less a tuxedo there. That thought hadn't occurred to Violet, however. She surged ahead, eyeballing the displays for just the right look.

It didn't take long for Aidan to mentally check out of the situation. After eyeing a pair of sunglasses he liked and nearly choking at the cost, he leaned against the wall and let his eyes glaze over while she shopped. He focused on her movements as she sauntered back and forth in a tight black pencil skirt that hugged her curves. The sway of her hips was hypnotizing, sending his mind into a full-fledged fantasy that included that skirt up around her hips and a mess of previously folded clothes on the nearby display scattered on the floor.

"Aidan?" she said in a cross tone a few minutes later.

He snapped out of it, realizing it was her beautiful irritated face, and not her ass, that was front and center at the moment. "Yes?"

"I already have a dress to wear to the party," she said. "I came here to help you find something nice to wear and you're not paying any attention to me. I need your input to find something that will work."

"How about you find me a suit with fewer than four digits in the price and I'll wear it?" he challenged. Pushing off from the wall with his shoulder, he strolled over to where Violet was standing with her arms crossed. "I don't know what kind of people typically come to the Niarchos Foundation for help, but I assure you I wouldn't be asking for money if I could lay out four grand for a tuxedo I'll wear one night."

Violet looked at him with concern lining her brow. "This night is important for you, Aidan. You're going to meet the people that will help you make Molly's House a success. They need to have confidence in you, and part of that is looking the part."

"I want to look competent. I don't want to look like I'm skimming from my own charity to line my pockets."

"Think of it this way. A nice, quality suit is a good investment. If you pick the right one, you'll be able to wear it your whole life."

"I'll be wearing it every damn day, Violet, because I'll have to sell all my other clothes to pay for it."

She sighed and twisted her lips in thought. Reaching out to a nearby rack, she pulled a sleeve toward her to glance at the price tag then let it drop. Turning back to Aidan, she narrowed her gaze. "We're getting you a suit. It's my treat. I insist."

Aidan held out his hands to fend off her misplaced generosity. "Oh, no. No, no, no. You are not my fairy godmother, Violet, and I'm not letting you buy me a suit for the ball. Absolutely not. I'll wear sweatpants to the gala before I let you do that." He meant it. It was one thing for Molly's House to be a charity case for the foundation. He wasn't about to be her personal charity case, no matter how badly she wanted to give him a makeover.

"I can afford it. Let me do this for you. As a thank-you for letting us stay with you at your apartment."

Aidan could feel a surge of irritation rise up his neck making him tug at the collar of his shirt. He was regretting mentioning his need of a tuxedo almost the moment he'd said it. The light had come on in her eyes and he knew he was in trouble. "Violet, you have more money than some small countries. I get that. I also get that you are a thoughtful person and you like helping people when you can. But I need you to look at this from my perspective."

"And how is that?"

Aidan crossed his arms over his chest to keep from curling his hands into fists of frustration.

"I'm a grown-ass man, Violet. I own my own business. I run my own life. I'm not used to anyone having a say in what I do or how I do it. I brought you along for your opinion. I certainly don't want or need someone picking out my clothes, much less paying for them. Would you have done that for your ex? Treated him like your Pygmalion project? Clean him up so he's suitable to go out in public?"

"Of course not," Violet argued.

"Because he didn't need to be cleaned up, right? He was already the perfect match your parents loved." Aidan shook his head and turned away. He needed to walk away from this before he said something he would regret. "I need some air."

Turning on his heel, Aidan headed for the exit and out onto Fifth Avenue. He pushed through the throngs of shoppers and tourists, hoping that the sounds of the city would block out the pounding of blood in his ears. When he got about a block from the store, he sat down on the edge of a planter and took a deep breath.

A few moments later, Violet sat down beside him without speaking. "I'm sorry," she said at last. "I'm not trying to change you or clean you up, and I don't want you to think that I am."

Aidan didn't say anything. He was too frustrated to answer her right now. He knew he wasn't a clean-cut, upper-class guy like she was used to. He didn't go to prep school or grow up with a trust fund. He went to a small state college on a scholarship and a prayer, trying to mold himself into a new and improved version of Aidan, but in truth, he didn't really like that Aidan. That was why it had been so easy to walk away from the advertising firm. He never felt like he fit in there, something his ex-fiancée did little to help him get through.

"I forget sometimes that people react to my money differently. Some ignore it. Some are more than happy to help me spend it on them or anyone else. Some are almost repelled by it. I try to do the best things I can with my inheritance, and that means helping people when they need it. But the last thing I want to do is use it in a way that makes you feel uncomfortable. So forget it. Buy your own damn suit."

When Aidan turned to look at her, she was smiling. "Fine. I will," he said, matching her smile.

"Fine!" She laughed and turned back to the traffic going by.

"I just need a new suit, Violet," he said after a few moments. "Just a suit. Basic black. Nothing fancy."

"Okay. Can we try again?"

Aidan shrugged. Despite his irritation, he did still need something to wear. "Yeah."

They stood up and when they turned around,

they were standing outside of Bergdorf Goodman. "Let's try in here," she said. "They have a variety of brands and even some ready-to-wear pieces that might work."

He reluctantly followed her into the store. They wandered through the displays, but he still didn't see anything that would suit her taste in his budget.

It wasn't until Violet caught a glimpse of a sales associate walking past them. "Excuse me?"

The man stopped and turned to them both with a polite smile. He was wearing a suit that probably cost more than either man made in a month, but that was a perk of working there, Aidan supposed. "Yes, can I help you find anything?"

"Actually, yes. Is there an area where you have any suits or suit pieces marked down? Maybe an end-of-season section?"

"We have a few things. Please follow me." The man with a name tag that said Marcus led them to the back corner of the men's formalwear section where there were a few pieces hanging. "This is all we have marked down in the store."

From Aidan's vantage point, he already knew it wasn't going to work. There was a camel-colored sport coat, a black corduroy blazer two sizes too large for him and a couple dress shirts. This wasn't exactly the type of place to have a sale. Those kind of things would be shipped out to an outlet store or discount retailer, not hanging in plain sight at the flagship Manhattan store. This was Fifth Avenue. It hurt the luxury branding to mark things down. Aidan knew that much from his years in marketing.

Violet looked over the selection and then turned back to the salesman with the sweetest smile he'd ever seen grace her lovely face. She wanted something, and he could tell she was determined to find a way to get it on Aidan's terms.

"I know this is a strange question, but do you ever get suit returns? I know with the custom tailoring you do here it might not happen very often, but I was hoping to find something for my friend. You see, Marcus, we're both involved in a charity organization that's hosting a black-tie event for some very important donors. As much as I'd love to just pick out the latest style and let your tailors start measuring him, it's probably going to be out of our budget."

Marcus listened to her speak, nodding in consideration. "What kind of charity is this for?"

"I'm opening a transitional home called Molly's House," Aidan chimed in. "It's designed to help alcoholics transition from rehab back into real life by giving them a safe space and the tools they need to cope with their new sobriety. I'm trying to make a good impression on our potential donors, but the young lady's taste far exceeds my budget. I understand if there's nothing in the store that will work for what I need."

Marcus looked thoughtfully over their shoulders for a moment and then held up his finger. "I actually might have something." He disappeared into a doorway marked Private and came out a few minutes later with a black Tom Ford suit bag in his hand.

"This was a custom tuxedo order. We've called the client repeatedly to pick it up over the last month and this morning, he finally called back to tell us that he'd changed his mind about the order. It's a Tom Ford slim-fit mohair and wool-blend tuxedo. You would need some additional alterations, but it might work for what you want."

Aidan watched the man unzip the bag. Inside was a sharp, black tuxedo with a black satin lapel and bow tie. He turned in time to see Violet's eyes light up at the sight of it. He knew from the description alone that she'd love it. "How much?" he asked. He didn't want to try it on and have her fall in love with something he still couldn't afford.

Marcus eyed the paperwork attached to the suit bag and did a little mental math. "Normally this is something we couldn't sell, since it was a custom order. We'd either allow one of our employees to use their discount on it or pass it along to the outlet locations, but for you, I think I can make an exception. Would seventy-five percent off make it doable for you?"

Aidan glanced at the paperwork and realized that he was about to get an amazing deal on a designer tuxedo. It was more than he wanted to spend, even then, but the quality was well worth the investment. "Are you serious?" he asked.

Marcus smiled and nodded. "I am. Why don't we take you back to try it on? I'll get one of our tailors to mark it up for you and you can pick it up later this week."

"Okay." Aidan followed him back, leaving Violet in the area outside the dressing rooms.

Once they were alone, he turned to Marcus as he hung the suit in one of the private rooms. "Is this suit really supposed to be marked down that much?"

"Probably not," Marcus said. "But my step-father is a recovering alcoholic. I appreciate the work you're trying to do, and if I can help you look good doing it, I will."

Seven

"Where are you two headed?"

The following day, Aidan was leaving his building with Knox in his stroller when he ran into Violet coming in. "Hey. I didn't expect you to be off so early today."

"Well, I decided I could stop and take some work home or stay in the office and work until ten. I opted to leave for my own sanity. Are you guys headed out with Tara?"

Aidan laughed. "No, I gave Tara the afternoon off. She mentioned needing to run a few errands. Since I'm off today, I thought I'd take Knox to the park so Tara could do what she needed without hauling the baby everywhere with her."

Violet stiffened and straightened the laptop bag on her shoulder. He could tell that she didn't like the idea of him having the baby on his own, despite how often he'd interacted with Knox while they'd shared his apartment. "Since you're home early, would you like to join us?" he offered to defuse the tension.

"A trip to the park would be nice," she said, obviously trying not to act like she was afraid of him handling their infant without help. "Can you give me a minute to run upstairs and change?"

"Absolutely. We'll be right here."

Violet went upstairs and returned about ten minutes later, dressed for the park. She'd pulled her dark hair up into a ponytail and put on a pair of tight jeans and a little T-shirt that highlighted her curves. It was casual and clingy, and he enjoyed the look far more than any of the stuffy outfits she seemed to wear at work each day.

They walked a few blocks to the nearest park in a relatively comfortable silence. Once they arrived, they continued around the shady path circling the playground area. Knox was still far too young to play at the park, but Aidan liked the idea of getting him out of the apartment and into what little nature Manhattan provided.

Knox looked up at the canopy of trees and sky overhead and took everything in with wide eyes.

He thoughtfully sucked on his Iron Man pacifier, content with his smooth ride in the stroller.

Aidan smiled down at his son, then looked out at the other people around the park. "Nothing but nannies," he pointed out with an irritated edge to his voice.

Violet just shrugged off his observation. "It's the middle of a weekday. Most people are at work and that means a nanny has to take them, or they'd be in school or day care."

Aidan understood the practicality of it, but that didn't mean he liked it. "I get it. There aren't many stay-at-home moms these days. And Tara has won me over, no question. I just worry that these kids are growing up without the kind of parental attention and affection they need to be well-rounded and emotionally healthy adults."

Violet turned to him with a curious cock of her head. "Do you find me to be well-rounded and emotionally healthy?"

Despite the alarm bells going off in his head, he knew he had to answer honestly if he was ever going to convince Violet to raise their son any differently. "Not really. You and your parents definitely have issues. I don't know you well enough to see how that flows into your daily life, but I've already seen evidence of it in our relationship."

Violet stopped walking and planted her hands on her hips. "Like what?"

"Like your drive for perfection in yourself and in others. Your constant unfounded worry that you're not going to make the right decision. I mean, I can tell you that you're the closest thing to perfection I've ever encountered and you won't believe me. You'll only hear your parents' criticisms. I don't understand why their opinion is so important."

Violet sighed and her gaze shifted to a far-off corner of the park. "Their opinion is important because I was always vying for their attention as a child. You're right, I was with nannies over ninety-five percent of my childhood. My parents were always working or traveling or doing any number of things that took them far away from me. I had to be the best at everything I did just so they would take notice of me, but it never seemed like enough for them. I was valedictorian in high school, I went to the college they wanted, I got the degree they wanted, I dated the man they wanted…they still weren't happy. Until the day I walked into Murphy's Pub, I was living a life of their choosing, not mine."

Aidan didn't understand Violet's parents at all and he didn't look forward to the day he'd have to interact with them. They might be Knox's grandparents, but he certainly wasn't going to let them belittle and micromanage his son the way they did with her. "They should be thrilled to have a daughter like you, no matter who you date or what you do."

Violet turned back to him and studied his face for a moment as though she didn't believe his words. He couldn't understand how she could question them.

"Despite what you might think, I don't want to raise Knox the way I was raised. Yes, I have a nanny to help me while he's small, but I have no intention of ever handing my child over while I go globetrotting. I will be there for every day of my son's life. And I want you to be there, too."

Her expression was gravely serious as she looked in his eyes. Up until this point, Aidan wasn't entirely sure that was how she felt. She seemed agreeable enough to including him in Knox's life, but it had only been a couple weeks. They'd just gotten back the positive paternity test results they were both anticipating, and looked over a draft custody arrangement with her attorney. Would she feel the same way months or years from now? When her parents and the rest of Manhattan society found out Knox's father was a poor nobody?

"I mean it," she continued. "Regardless of what happens between the two of us, I want you to be as big of a part of your son's life as you can. Knox deserves that. And you do, too."

Violet reached out and covered his hand with her own as it gripped the stroller handle. Just like at the office, her touch was warm and comforting, reminding him how long it had been since someone had touched him so tenderly. Perhaps since his mom died. His gaze dropped uncomfortably to her hand as he tried not to get overly emotional in the public moment they were sharing.

"Thank you," he said at last. "My father was never around, either. He was always at the bar or sleeping off a bender. I'm not sure whether he opened the bar because he was an alcoholic or if he became an alcoholic because he owned a bar, but the result was the same. He was wasted or hungover most of the time. He never did any of the things a dad is supposed to do with his son. He never even came to one of my ball games in high school. My mom did her best to make up for it, but there was only so much she could do."

"I can't imagine you ever being that kind of father, Aidan. You've known your son for such a short time and yet you adore him. Anyone can see that. You're not going to cast him aside like your father did to you."

"Did you know that's why I don't drink?"

Violet frowned. "I hadn't noticed that, although it makes perfect sense."

"I can't even tell you what a beer tastes like, only how it smells. I was always too afraid of being like him. I worried one drink would turn into ten and the next thing I knew, I'd be in as deep as he was. I couldn't do that to myself or to my mother. She'd already been through so much with my dad."

"The halfway house will help a lot of people."

"It was my mother's idea, really. Dad tried rehab twice and it worked fairly well at first, but once he came home and went back to work, he'd settle back into his bad habits. Even if he didn't work in a bar he would've had trouble. She always said that he needed more than twenty-eight days. He needed a transitional place to help him adjust to his sobriety in his old, comfortable situations. She hated not being able to stop my father from destroying himself, and eventually that's what he did. He died of liver failure about three years ago. That's why I quit my job at the advertising agency and took over Murphy's."

"Wait. You worked at an advertising agency?"

Aidan frowned. Had he not told her that story? He supposed they had barely scratched the surface in their discussions. "Yeah. I was an advertising executive for about five years after graduating from college. I'd worked on a few successful campaigns for some big accounts and was being fast-tracked at the firm. It was certainly a different life than the one I live now."

"Do you ever miss the work?"

"I hate to disappoint you, but no, I don't. I was trying to better myself and I realized that it didn't make me any happier than I was when I was poor. In truth, I was miserable. Successful and miserable. Running my father's bar isn't the most important or well-paying job in the world, but I like my employees and my clientele. I enjoy going in most days. I like being there when people need someone to talk to. It's a completely different kind of experience each day and I like that."

Violet seemed flabbergasted by their whole discussion. "I don't know why I thought you'd always worked at the bar. Advertising…" She shook her head. "I guess we have a lot to learn about each other."

"We do. I guess it just hasn't come up, but I thought you knew. That's why I've got that nice apartment in Hell's Kitchen. I used my advertising bonuses as a down payment or I couldn't afford to live in it now."

"You own your place? I didn't realize that, either." Violet frowned and Aidan understood why.

"We've done things a little backward, I have to admit."

They turned and started walking back down the path through the park. The more Aidan thought about it, the more he wanted to do things right with Violet. Their relationship was all out of order. They'd had a baby first, then lived together, albeit temporarily. They knew very little about each other's pasts. They might have an emotional connection, but they'd flunk out on *The Newlywed Game*. It was all backward and he wanted to go back to the beginning and have a relationship reset. "I think there's something you and I need to do. Something important."

"What's that?" she asked with a curious expression on her face.

"A real, honest-to-goodness date with food and conversation and getting to know one another. Violet, would you be interested in going out on a date with me?"

This was not what Violet had in mind when Aidan said he wanted to go on a date. She was picturing a nice restaurant, candlelight, maybe a walk through Central Park. The usual. She should've known that with Aidan their date would be anything but the usual. Instead, it was three in the afternoon and she, along with literally fifty thousand other people, was walking into Yankee Stadium to watch a home game against the Pittsburgh Pirates.

It wasn't that she didn't like baseball. She did. The foundation even had seats in the Delta

SKY360 Suites that she made use of from time to time, especially when donors needed to be wooed. But it just wasn't what she was expecting when she got asked out. She should've known something was up when Aidan said to be ready at two and to dress casual.

At the same time, the light of excitement in Aidan's eyes made it all worth it. Baseball was important to him. She'd seen the trophy from the state championship he'd won in high school at his apartment. The first gift he gave to his son was a Yankees jersey and a baseball mitt no larger than an orange. She didn't even know they made mitts that small. So coming to see a game was obviously an important experience for him to share with Violet.

She tried to keep that in mind as she stopped at Aidan's side while he looked down at their tickets. Then she realized she could give him a new way to experience the game. "Would you like to go see if anyone is sitting in the foundation box?"

Aidan looked at the section where their tickets were and shrugged with indifference. "I forgot you had those. It's up to you."

Violet tried to hide her disappointment. She thought he would be more excited to get the chance to sit in their swanky private box. "It's awfully hot right now. At the very least we can sit in the air-conditioning and have a private restroom. I thought you might like it."

He nodded. "Our seats are in the direct sunlight. If you're already hot, it might be a good idea to check it out and maybe we can move down closer to the field once the sun sets. Otherwise I will have wasted these thirty-dollar tickets," he added with a smile.

Violet met his smile, hopeful he wasn't offended by her suggestion. In truth, she'd never sat in the regular seats. Her father never let her. He was a big baseball fan. That was half the reason they had the box seats. The foundation was just a good excuse for him to get one. It was one thing he and Aidan would actually have in common if she ever introduced them.

Unfortunately it wouldn't be enough to satisfy her ever-critical father.

So far, as best Violet could tell, nothing he'd acquired on this earth could satisfy her father. Aidan was doomed to failure in that regard, whether he was a crown prince or a Lower East Side bartender.

She didn't want to worry about that today. Today, her parents were in Istanbul, and she just wanted to enjoy her afternoon with Aidan. She led him around the stadium to the stairs that would take them up to the executive boxes.

"Good afternoon, Eddie," Violet said with a

smile as she approached the security guard who policed the east entrance to the boxed seats. She brought more than her share of donors to games here and recognized the regular guard. "Is anyone using the Niarchos Foundation box today? I wasn't sure if Daddy had let one of his friends use it or not and I forgot to check before I left."

The large, muscular man with dark brown skin and kind eyes looked down at his tablet and shook his head. "Not today, Miss Niarchos. Will you and your guest be joining us for the game?"

"For a while, I think, until it cools down."

"I'll let the servers know."

"Are there many VIPs up here today?" Violet asked. Sometimes there were actors, politicians or rock stars roaming around these halls and taking in a game.

"More important than you?" Eddie asked with a smile. "Of course not."

Violet playfully smacked Eddie on the arm. "Flattery will get you everything." She turned back to Aidan and took his hand. "Come on."

It didn't take long to reach the Niarchos Foundation box. Just slightly to the right of home plate, they had one of the best views of the park. They went inside, passing the private catering and lounge seating area and approaching the large wall of windows and rows of seats that held over twenty people for each game. When they did big events here, the room would be filled with people munching on platters of catered food and bottles of imported wine and beer. At the moment, the large space was silent and empty.

"It's a shame we don't use this more. Occasionally we auction off use of the box for charity events or bring donors as a perk, but more often than not, it's empty like this. We should coordinate with children's groups like the scouts or contact the Make-A-Wish Foundation to let them use it. It's such a waste."

Violet looked out the window where the two ball teams were still warming up on the field. The stadium seats were pretty full now, so it would be time to start soon. "Well, what do you think?" she asked. "Do you like it? We don't have to stay up here if you don't."

When she got no response, she turned to see Aidan looking wide-eyed and overwhelmed behind her. "Aidan? What's the matter?"

He pulled his gaze away from the stunning view of the ballfield and turned to her. "This is, uh, nice."

Violet frowned. "You don't like it."

"No, no. I mean, it's very swanky. I should be thrilled to get the chance to sit in a private box, knowing how much it costs to reserve one for a game, much less a season. But I don't know… it feels like something is lost. Almost like we're watching it on a television from home. It's impersonal."

A tap at the door was followed by the entrance of a server wearing the standard all-black uniform for the VIP suites. "Good afternoon. Can I bring you anything before the game starts?"

Violet looked to Aidan, hoping perhaps the perks might win him over. "Would you like to order something? They have a full bar, lots of food options…even a sushi chef."

"Are you serious?"

With his Yankees cap pulled down over his eyes, it was hard to read Aidan, but Violet was pretty sure he wasn't impressed with the sushi. "I think we're okay right now, thank you," she said, dismissing their in-suite server.

Once the door clicked shut, Aidan crossed his arms over his chest and chuckled. "Is this where you sit every time you come to a game?"

"Yes," she said. "Although sometimes we go down to the sky bar."

"Where you drink martinis and eat sushi while enjoying America's game?"

He was making fun of her. Violet wasn't used to that. Most people kissed her rear end because of her money. Others just ignored it. But Aidan, he was goading her because of it. "We have this box. Why wouldn't I sit up here?"

Aidan just shook his head. He looked around

the room one last time and held out his hand. "Come on. You're coming with me and you're going to have a real game experience."

Violet hesitated. She wasn't sure why.

"Come on, this is a date and I planned for us to sit in cheap seats, drink sodas and share nachos while we scream at the umpire. I don't want to sit up here in the sterile, fancy place where the rich can avoid dealing with the rest of us."

"That's not why—" she started to argue, but Aidan cut her off.

"Come on, Violet. We're going to start by buying you a Yankees shirt."

Violet took his hand and before she knew it, she was in a section of the stadium she'd never seen before. She was wearing a brand-new Yankees T-shirt blinged out with rhinestones—her requirement—and sitting between Aidan and a family there with their young kids.

He was right. There was definitely a different feel watching the game down here. You could feel the energy of the crowd, smell the roasted peanuts and freshly mowed grass, and actually see the players as more than tiny white blurs. Aidan got them both cold lemonades they drank from plastic cups, then they had hot dogs and shared a huge container of nachos.

When one of the Yankees players hit a home run, she leaped from her seat in excitement with everyone else, loudly cheering for the team. And when the seventh-inning stretch rolled around, she sang "Take Me Out to the Ballgame" with the whole stadium.

By the top of the ninth, the sun had set and bright lights shone down on them. The game was a blowout and some people had already started to mill out, but she wasn't ready to leave yet. She was full of greasy ballpark food and she couldn't stop smiling at Aidan.

"So what do you think?" he asked her. "Shall we go back up to the VIP seats? Get some sushi?"

She winced at him and shook her head. "No. You were right. This was a lot more fun. I can't believe I've never seen a game from down here. I don't know why my father wouldn't let me."

Aidan's auburn brow went up in surprise. "Let you? You about bit my head off when I even suggested that someone else dictate what you could or couldn't do."

Violet sighed. "My father is different. He's old-school Greek. He didn't really want me to do much of anything but get married to a nice Greek boy and have lots of Greek babies."

"You're just a rebel, then," Aidan said with a grin. "Having Irish babies, eating nachos in the cheap seats…what's next?"

He was right. She was being quite the rebel lately and Aidan was the cause. She liked it. And she liked him. He encouraged her to stretch her wings, broaden her narrow view of the world and live a little. He roused feelings in her she'd never experienced before and she wanted more. More of him, more of the sensations he could coax out of her trembling body. Violet looked up at the VIP boxes and grinned with the wicked idea that came to mind.

"On second thought, I think we do need to make a trip back up to the Niarchos box before we leave today."

"Why? Did you leave something up there?"

She shook her head and leaned in to him to let her soft lips brush against his earlobe. She bit gently at it, feeling a shiver run through his whole body that had nothing to do with the cold. "Ever wanted to have sex in Yankee Stadium?" she whispered.

Aidan pulled away in surprise and looked at her with one deviously arched brow. He studied her face for a moment before a passionate fire lit in his eyes. "I hadn't ever considered the possibility, but now that you mention it…" his arm wrapped around her waist and tugged her closer to him "…abso-frickin-lutely."

He stood suddenly and offered her his hand. Violet accepted, and they made their way back to the VIP box. The desire for him built inside of her with every step they took. Once they were inside the private suite, she locked the door and pressed her back against it.

"Time to score."

Eight

Aidan paused on the sidewalk outside of Violet's building with one piece of luggage slung over his shoulder and another on wheels behind him. Tara and Knox had already gone upstairs, and Violet was taking a bag from the cab driver as he pulled it out of the back of the van.

"Are you sure everything is done right?" he asked again. The contractor had called to tell them this morning that her apartment was done and she could move back in. A day early. Apparently the damage hadn't been as extensive structurally as they thought, so they'd only needed to do cosmetic repairs. He supposed he should be happy for Violet and Knox's sake, but he wasn't. He'd thought he had another day living with them as a family and with one phone call, he was helping her pack.

"Yes, Aidan," Violet said with a sigh that told him she was tired of him asking. He may have pestered her a *few* times since she said they could go back to the apartment.

Who could blame him?

He wasn't ready for things to go back to the way they were before the flood. It had been like a jump start to their relationship. Suddenly they were together all the time in a way that would've taken weeks or months to happen otherwise. He liked waking up to Knox's giggles in the living room and going to bed with Violet in his arms. Sharing meals, taking a grocery shopping trip together. It was the simple things that he enjoyed the most.

It was almost like they were…a family. A real family, not that coparenting thing they'd agreed to with her attorney.

Violet set down the bag on the sidewalk and turned to him. "We're not leaving the country, Aidan. We're just moving back across town. You know where to find us." She planted a kiss on his lips and patted his cheek reassuringly.

"I know that." And practically, he did. He just didn't like the idea of it. He wanted to keep his family together, but he was afraid he'd scare her away if he said something like that aloud. It was too soon. And yet he felt certain about it. More certain than he had ever felt with Iris.

Just then, Aidan turned and noticed a man coming down the sidewalk waving at them. Or presumably to Violet since Aidan had never seen the man before.

"Violet? I think that guy wants to talk to you."

She took a step back from him and turned, her happy expression crumbling when she saw the man coming closer. "Damn it," she swore. "I've been back here for five minutes and he's shown up already."

"Violet!" the man shouted as he approached before Aidan could ask who it was.

He had a pretty good guess. The man was wearing a fancy suit and a smile that came across to Aidan as extremely insincere. Like a car salesman. The kind who sold Jaguars, perhaps, but still a car salesman. Especially when he brushed past Aidan without a second glance and placed a hand on Violet's upper arm.

"There you are, dear. I've been looking for you for days, but no one answered when I knocked."

Violet pulled away from his touch. "I haven't been home this week, Beau. My apartment flooded and they've been doing renovations for the past few days."

"What? Flooded? Why didn't you call me to deal with all of this?"

Violet looked irritated, frowning as she planted her hands on her hips. Aidan couldn't fathom how a man who had been engaged to her at one point would be so clueless about how she responded to him.

"Why would I call you? We're not together anymore. We haven't been a couple for six months. And besides that, I can handle this on my own. I don't need you to come and deal with things for me."

"Of course you could, my pet, but where have you been all week?" Beau asked, ignoring that it wasn't his business and Violet didn't seem interested in talking to him.

"She's been staying with me," Aidan interjected. Beau had already touched Violet without her permission, used pet names, questioned her competence and completely ignored Aidan's presence. It was time for all of that to change.

Beau finally turned toward him as though he'd just noticed Aidan standing there. "Oh. I thought he was your cab driver."

Aidan started to tense for a fight, but a cautioning hand from Violet stopped him. "Quit being so rude, Beau. You knew full well that he was here with me. I'm not going to just stand here while you show up unannounced, question everything

I do and then be disrespectful to my guest. Why don't you tell me what it is you want so you can go and I can finish moving back upstairs?"

Beau turned to Aidan with a disgusted look, as though he were somehow responsible for Violet's new backbone. "I just wanted to say hi and see how you were. You haven't been returning my calls."

"Hi. I'm fine, thank you. And I haven't returned your calls because we're not dating any longer."

"I know we're not but—"

"No buts, Beau. I made it very clear when the paternity test came back, but you and my parents don't seem to want to listen. So here's what you need to know—I'm seeing someone else now. End of story."

"Him?" Beau said with a thumb jerked in Aidan's direction.

"Yes," she answered matter-of-factly.

"And just who is he, huh?"

"Knox's father." Violet said the words proudly, startling Aidan.

So far, she'd seemed fairly hesitant for people to know about their relationship, especially where Knox was concerned. He understood that things were new between them, and that she wanted to feel more comfortable before the world poked its nose into their business. Apparently she was feeling more comfortable. Or at least angry enough with Beau overstepping in her business to want to throw that factoid in his face.

"I thought you didn't know who his father was."

"I didn't know. If I had, I certainly wouldn't have led you and everyone else on the entire nine months. But I've gotten some of my memory back from that lost week."

"Some? Not all of it?" Beau asked with a concerned furrow of his brow.

"No, not all of it. Just the part where I met Aidan. We've since reunited. That's all of my business you're going to be privy to from here on out."

Beau's worried expression faded as he crossed his arms over his chest. "Do your parents know about…*him*?" The word almost seemed to taste bad in his mouth as he said it.

It made Aidan want to glance down at what he was wearing to see how bad he looked. He had on nice jeans and a fitted T-shirt with the name of his bar on it. He certainly wasn't dressing up to haul her stuff back to the apartment. And yet her jerk of an ex seemed to think he was less than worthy of Violet.

Maybe so, but her opinion was the only one that mattered. At the moment, she seemed to think he was good enough. She didn't seem the slightest bit embarrassed to announce who he was and that they were dating. He was surprised, especially considering that someone like Beau could take that information straight to her parents or family friends.

"Not that it's any of your business, but no, I haven't spoken to my parents about it yet. They haven't been stateside in a while. But I will when they return. And if you rush home and tell them, Beau, I will make your life extremely difficult, do you understand?"

For a moment Beau's macho demeanor seemed to crumble a bit under Violet's threat. Then he recovered and shrugged it off. "Like I want to spend my precious time gossiping about who my ex is sleeping with. If it's not me, I really don't care. Call me when you regain your senses," he said, turning to walk away without giving Aidan a second glance.

Violet and Aidan both stood together watching Beau stroll casually down the sidewalk, disappearing into a crowd. "That guy is a piece of work," Aidan noted. "If you weren't dating me, I'd question your taste in men."

"I'd question my taste in men, too, except I didn't really choose Beau. We grew up together and it was always just sort of expected that we would get married one day. If I'd been born a hundred years earlier, our marriage would've been arranged. Now, my parents just used social pressures to get us together."

"I don't know why they'd want you with that jerk."

Violet lifted the handle of the bag and started toward the door of her building. "I guess because our families are old friends, we're around the same age, he's from a good family, and of course, he's Greek. They're not good reasons, but they're reasons. I've always said we were better on paper than in real life."

Aidan just shook his head and followed her inside. "Well, if I was your father, the most important thing to me would be how he treated you. And considering the state you were in the night you came into Murphy's, I'd say he wasn't treating you well at all."

Violet paused in the marble and brass lobby and turned to him. "Did I tell you anything that night? Like I just told Beau, I still don't remember everything about that week. Just you. I don't know why I was upset or in the bar that night."

Aidan realized they hadn't really discussed her memory loss in quite a while. At first, he'd considered it a convenient excuse, but the way she spoke about it now, he was more convinced that she really had lost her memory. "You didn't say. Actually, what you said was that you didn't want to talk about it. Just that your boyfriend was, quote, 'a dick' and you wanted to forget about every-thing for a while."

Violet rolled her eyes and turned toward the elevators. "Be careful what you wish for, huh?"

The apartment was in fine shape. If it wasn't for the faint smell of drying paint, Violet almost wouldn't be able to tell anything had happened in her kitchen. Knox went down happily for his af-ternoon nap while Violet, Aidan and Tara worked on unpacking their suitcases. Violet started a load of laundry and then she and Aidan settled on the couch in the living room with glasses of iced tea.

"That guy was a real ass," Aidan said. Even though over an hour had passed since Beau walked off, they both knew exactly who he was referring to.

Violet was well aware that her ex-fiancé was an ass. He may not have deserved Violet cheating on him and having another man's baby, but he wasn't the right man for her by any stretch of the imagi-nation. "I know. He does have moments where I can see the guy that charmed me in college, but they became few and far between as we got older. What scares me the most is that I almost married him. I was quite upset at first when I realized I was pregnant, because I knew what it meant for me. Things had been great with Beau since my accident, but I knew it wouldn't last. Being pregnant meant my chance to walk away from the relationship was over. Having his baby meant getting married. End of story. At least as far as our family and friends were concerned.

"I delayed the wedding by insisting I wanted to wait until after the baby was born. Everyone thought I was just being vain about looking thin on my wedding day, but the truth was that I was looking for any reason to put it off. Then Knox arrived in all his redheaded glory and saved me from having to go through with it. I insisted on a paternity test even though Beau was pushing to be put on the birth certificate and have the baby take his last name. I refused. Something hadn't felt right, and when the results came back, I knew what it was at last. But if Knox had taken after me with dark hair and eyes I might never have questioned if Beau was his father and married him."

She shook her head, shaking off the shudder that ran through her at the mere thought of being Mrs. Beau Rosso. Her pregnancy had been such a confusing time for her, although she'd never spoken to anyone about her concerns. She'd blamed it on the accident at first, but still, she'd questioned it. She'd lain in bed at night looking at her gigantic engagement ring, feeling Knox move in her belly and wishing she knew why it didn't feel right. Something had bothered her about Beau since the accident and she couldn't put her finger on what it was. She'd hoped that the return of her memory would solve the question, but the answer hadn't popped up along with all her memories of the time with Aidan. Amnesia was an incredibly frustrating illness, like having a word on the tip of your tongue but being unable to voice it.

"I almost married the wrong person, too. It happens more than you'd think. I guess we're just lucky we figured it out before we took the plunge."

Violet turned to look at Aidan in surprise. He'd never mentioned a fiancée before, but then again, they hadn't spent much time rehashing their old relationships aside from the thing with Beau. "May I ask what happened?"

Aidan sighed and propped his head in his hand. "Do you want the long version of the story or the short version?"

"The long version." She sensed some underlying animosity in Aidan and she didn't know where it came from. He didn't really seem to like people with money and took a lot of offense to how much Violet had. His attitude certainly wasn't the result of anything she'd done, per se, but she could feel it sometimes. She wondered now if this wasn't where it originated.

"Back when I was working at the advertising agency, I started seeing a woman named Iris. She was a corporate attorney I met at a party. We were together for about three years before I decided

to propose. I knew she had particular tastes—
by that I mean expensive ones—but at the time
I didn't mind. I was trying to better my situation
and in my mind, part of that was dating a high-
class girl with high-class tastes. I could afford
to indulge her, and buying her things made her
happy. I thought that was just how it worked. My
mistake was thinking that our relationship was
based on more than that."

Violet felt her stomach start to ache. She already knew how this story would end because
she'd met Iris before. Not his Iris, but women like
her whose loyalty to a relationship lasted only as
long as the money did. When it dried up, they
went in search of a new source.

"Anyway, so when my father died and I decided to quit my job in advertising to run Murphy's, I was stupid enough to think that Iris would
stand by me. She didn't. In fact, she called me a
damn fool and left me almost immediately for one
of the senior partners at my advertising firm. It all
happened so quickly, I had to wonder if she hadn't
been seeing him long before all that happened."

"That's awful," Violet said, even knowing what
was coming. Breaking up with Aidan was one
thing but throwing it in his face like that was just
cruel. A woman like that didn't deserve a man
like Aidan. It made Violet wonder if even she was
good enough for him. After all, she'd cheated on

Beau with Aidan, hadn't she? It was completely out of character for Violet, and it frustrated her not knowing or understanding why she'd done it, but Knox was proof that she had. In that case, was she any better than Iris?

"How can you do that to someone you're supposed to love?" she asked instead. Perhaps her lukewarm feelings for Beau had been the cause of her infidelity. They had been arguing a lot at the time.

Aidan shrugged and sipped his tea thoughtfully. "She loved money more than me, I guess. Iris wouldn't even give me the engagement ring back after she broke it off, even though she knew I needed every penny I could get to bail out the bar. I should've known how screwed up her priorities were, but I find a lot of people in this town think just like her. The more they have, the more they love it. Need it. Are willing to do anything for it."

Violet didn't like the bitter tone his story had taken even though she understood why he would be upset. "I don't know that that's true. There are rich and greedy people everywhere. It doesn't mean everyone is like that, though."

"Isn't it true? I'll admit I'm jaded when it comes to rich people, but I have reason to be. With guys on Wall Street like Beau willing to do anything to turn a buck… Pharmaceutical companies willing to let my mom die because she couldn't afford their jacked-up prices on medication… Beau was even willing to claim a child he knew wasn't his just to…"

Violet sat at attention in her seat. "Just to what?"

Aidan shrugged. "I don't know. Maybe I'm wrong and he loved you and the baby no matter what. But my experience leads me to believe that he'd accept just about anything you threw his way if you'd marry him and he could get his hands on all your money."

She'd worried about that. It had always been a factor in the back of her mind whenever she dated anyone. Most men in her social circles knew how much she was worth, at least within a couple hundred million. Somehow, she'd hoped that growing up with Beau had negated that. She'd hoped his affections for her were sincere. And yet, when Aidan said the words out loud, she knew it was true. Beau wanted to land the billionaire heiress. He kept coming back around no matter what she did because he really didn't care what she did. He probably didn't even love her. He just wanted the lifestyle—the prestige—being her husband would provide. He and his family were well off, but not ridiculously rich the way the Niarchos family was. Marrying her would afford him private planes and yachts and going his whole life without working a day if he didn't want to. Love and mutual respect had nothing to do with it. That was not what she wanted her marriage to be based on.

"You might be right about Beau. And about Iris. We obviously aren't the best at choosing romantic partners. But I refuse to believe that everyone out there feels the same way. Money and status aren't everything."

Aidan chuckled at her observation. "Only people with money and status would say that. They say money problems are the number-one cause of break ups."

"No, I'm serious," Violet insisted. "Beau was all wrong for me. I know that now. But all my parents saw was a successful guy from a good family and they looked the other way at all his other flaws. While it's nice to be financially stable and well known in the community, it isn't the most important thing in a relationship. If it were, rich people would never divorce and they do all the time."

Aidan looked at her curiously. "So what do you think is the most important thing?"

Violet had thought about this a lot since she'd broken things off with Beau. She didn't want to make the same mistakes next time, so she'd really tried to identify what she wanted in a partner. "Chemistry and attraction can draw you together, but relationships need a solid foundation to last," she began. "That takes mutual trust, respect and caring for one another. You have to be able to count on your partner to be there when things get hard. To stand by your side when you lose the money and status like you did to run your father's bar. Those things, to me, are far more important than the other stuff. That's what I'm going to look for if I ever decide to get engaged again."

He leaned toward her with a smile that made her stomach flutter. "You mean a poor schmuck like me actually has a chance of winning the heart and hand of a rich, successful and beautiful woman like you?"

There was a light of jest in his eyes as he said the words, but she knew that inside, he wasn't kidding. Violet's chest ached at the thought that Aidan believed he wasn't good enough for her somehow. Why had he put her on a pedestal like that? It made her want to throttle Iris for making him feel like he was unworthy of her love.

"Of course you do," she said, reaching out to take his hand and squeeze it gently. The heat of his touch warmed her blood, making her suddenly flush in the relatively cool apartment. "I wouldn't have gotten involved with you once, much less twice, if you didn't have a chance. I'm not the kind to take physical connections lightly."

Aidan's gaze searched her face for a moment, and then he nodded, pulling his hand away from hers. "I'll keep that in mind," he said. "I'd better get going. Tonight is my last night off until the gala on Saturday. I've got a lot to get done before then."

They both stood, and Violet followed him to the front door. She understood he had things to do; she did, too, and yet, she hated the thought of him leaving. Normally, she was the kind of woman who liked having some alone time even in a relationship, but she found herself fighting the urge to fling her arms around his neck to keep him from going. She wasn't ready yet.

How had she gotten so attached to Aidan so quickly? In all the years she was with Beau, she'd never felt this way. "Stay," she said in a soft voice before she could overthink it.

He looked at her curiously with his hand on the doorknob. "After almost a week together, I thought you'd be sick of me by now."

"Me, too," Violet said with a smile. "But surprisingly, I'm not."

His hand dropped from the doorknob and he moved it to rest on her hip. He came in close to her, warming her body and wrapping her in the cocoon of his alluring scent. She wanted to press into him and pull him into her bedroom.

She wasn't sure how she was going to fall asleep without him in the bed beside her.

Violet pressed her face into his neck, feeling the warmth of his skin and the thrum of his pulse against her lips. "So stay," she whispered in his ear.

"Okay. You've twisted my arm."

Nine

The rest of the afternoon passed painfully slowly. Once Violet convinced Aidan to stay the night, it was a countdown to having him in her arms. She'd gotten used to falling asleep beside him and waking up with his scent on her pillowcase. They weren't keeping their relationship or Knox's parentage a secret from Tara any longer, but they weren't flaunting it in front of the nanny, either. That meant if Violet wanted a soft, slow kiss or a good hug, she had to wait for bedtime.

Although the kitchen was repaired, most of the cabinet contents were still in boxes in the dining room. Aidan ordered Chinese delivery while Violet fed Knox some baby cereal and mashed-up banana. The banana—at least what made it into his mouth—was a hit.

At bedtime, Aidan took his opportunity to put his son to bed. Violet watched from a distance as he went through the nightly routine he'd picked up from her while they'd stayed with him. A new diaper, pajamas and then a quick rock in the rocking chair together to settle Knox down. Sometimes Violet would tell Knox a story or sing him a song. When he was a little older, she would start reading to him. Aidan regaled his son with a story about the Yankees triumphing over the Phillies in the 2009 World Series. Knox lay in his arms, enthralled the entire time.

Watching the two of them together always turned her heart into butter. Violet wasn't entirely sure what it was really like to have a father—at least one who was involved in her life. Her bedtime had always involved a nanny, and if her parents were in town, perhaps a kiss on the forehead from her mother. But bedtime stories, baths and lullabies were not something she associated with her parents. Her father cared for her in his own way, but he just wasn't the demonstrative type. Her grandfather Stavros hadn't been the kind, either, although he'd warmed up to being a grandfather by the time she was born. Maybe someday her dad would soften with Knox, but when she was a child, it was likely all he knew how to be—firm and distant.

Violet knew that Aidan's father had problems drinking throughout Aidan's childhood, so it was possible he wasn't much of a hands-on father, either. The difference was that Aidan didn't use that as an excuse to be cold with his son. Instead, he went over and above, making sure he did better for Knox than his own father had done for him.

She appreciated that more than she even realized at first. Watching them together, she thanked her lucky stars for the twist of fate that brought her and Aidan together. She knew that even if Knox had been Beau's son, it wouldn't have been like this with him. He hadn't really been involved throughout the entire pregnancy. He blew off an ultrasound. Moped through the baby shower because he'd had to cancel a standing racquetball match for it. The idea of having a son appealed to him, but not the reality of it.

Aidan had a son dropped into his lap out of nowhere and he'd recovered beautifully. She got the feeling that going through her pregnancy with him would've been different, as well. Would he have rubbed her swollen ankles and gone out in search of her latest food craving? Probably so. Because he seemed to care about the people in his life. To Violet, that was more important than all the other things Beau supposedly had to offer her but Aidan didn't.

Knox nodded off in his father's arms. She watched as Aidan gently stood up, walked his son over to his crib and got him settled in.

"He's out cold," Aidan whispered when he turned and saw her watching him from the doorway. "How did I do, Mama? Did I pass the bedtime test?"

Violet smiled. She hadn't been watching him with that in mind, but she appreciated that he was trying to do everything right. "With flying colors."

"Do I get a reward for a job well done?" he asked with a devious arch of his brow.

"I think that could be arranged." Violet took his hand and led him across the hallway to her bedroom. Once inside, she shut her door and then pushed Aidan backward until he was sitting on the edge of the bed. With her gaze fixed on his, she slowly lowered herself down to her knees in front of him.

"Are you ready for your reward?" she asked with a coy smile.

"Oh, yeah."

Violet took her time, running her hands up and down his legs and stroking his thighs through his jeans before moving to his fly. She unbuttoned it and ran down the zipper, feeling his body tense beneath her touch. He helped her tug his jeans and black boxer briefs over his hips and down his legs. They went into a pile along with his shoes and the rest of his unnecessary clothes.

She'd barely touched Aidan and yet once he was naked, she realized he was already primed and ready for her. As she reached for his exposed desire, she heard his sharp intake of breath. He continued to hold his breath as she wrapped her fingers around his firm heat and gently stroked him until he let out a ragged burst of air from his lungs.

"Violet," he whispered with his eyes squeezed shut.

Feeling emboldened by his response, she brought him to her lips and enveloped him in the moist warmth. Aidan groaned aloud as she moved up and down the length of him, teasing at him with her tongue. He buried his fingers in her dark hair and bit at his bottom lip in an apparent effort to stay quiet.

Violet was determined to make that difficult for him. It was a reward, after all.

Working him over with her hands and mouth, she increased the pace until he was gritting his teeth. "Okay," he said, reaching out to grasp her wrist and still the torturous movements. "That... is about all I can take of that unless you want Tara to know way too much about us."

Violet giggled, but relinquished her hold on

him. "I'm sorry," she said in a pouty voice that proved she was anything but sorry.

"I bet you are." With one quick tug, he pulled her up off the floor, and she landed in a sprawled position on top of him. He held her tight to him even as she wiggled and tried to right herself. "Oh, no. You've had plenty of fun. It's your turn to shout," he said.

Rolling across the bed, Violet found herself on her back with Aidan pinning her arms to the mattress. He shifted his grip until he was holding both wrists in one of his massive hands over her head. He straddled her hips, using his free hand to push up her shirt. He shimmied it over her head and shoulders, leaving it tangled around her wrists. He unsnapped the front clasp of her bra and pushed the lacy blue cups out of his way to expose her tight, rosy nipples.

Violet gasped silently as he cupped her left breast in his hand and drew her into the warmth of his mouth. He sucked hard on her nipple until she squirmed and arched her back toward him. She was completely at his mercy now and not being able to move her arms made her feel even more vulnerable to him.

She liked it.

When he did finally let go, it was so he could slide her jeans and panties down her hips. With those gone, she used her newfound freedom to pull his face back down to her so she could kiss him at last. His lips collided hard with hers, matching the intensity that was building between them both. It had been less than a day since they'd shared a bed and yet it suddenly felt like weeks. Like Violet would be consumed by her need for him if she didn't have him right now.

Aidan seemed less inclined to rush tonight. Even as he kissed her, one hand roamed over her skin, eventually seeking out the heat between her thighs. He stroked her, dipping his fingers inside and rubbing the heel of his palm against her sensitive flesh. His mouth on hers muffled her cries as he made slow circles guaranteed to make her climax.

And climax she did. Her whole body was shaken with the pleasure that radiated through her. She'd never come so fast and so intensely before, but it was as though Aidan had mastered her body. She tore her mouth away from his to suck in a cool lungful of air and gasp with the force of her orgasm.

As she lay there, nearly incapable of moving, Aidan sought out a condom and returned to her side. As they came together, she felt her body responding to him again and Violet noticed a difference in their lovemaking. It had only been a week since they'd first come together at his apartment, and yet the newness had given way to the familiar and easy. Not that it was boring by any stretch, but that there was experience behind every touch and taste of each other's bodies. He knew exactly how to move and how to touch her to make her respond.

Violet had never been with a lover who focused on her pleasure the way he did. Even tonight, he had taken his reward and twisted it into an experience to satisfy them both. He didn't just give lip service to her needs, he genuinely prioritized them, just as he prioritized her in every aspect of his life.

Even as he groaned her name into her neck and held her body tight to his, she couldn't help but think of how special he made her feel. Like she and Knox were a priority in his life. Not his business or his money, his reputation or even himself. She'd never been loved like that before.

Is that what it was? Love?

If that was what she was feeling, Violet had never truly been loved by any man she'd been with in the past. At least not loved body and soul the way Aidan seemed to. He hadn't shared his feelings with her and she hadn't shared hers with him, but he certainly made her feel cherished and appreciated in a way that made her want to give a voice to her feelings.

She *was* in love with him.

It wasn't something she'd really thought about

before tonight, but the truth of it was clear. Their time together had been brief, but her heart and mind both knew what they wanted. They both wanted him.

She was absolutely, totally in love with Aidan.

The warm feeling in the center of her chest spread through her whole body. Like some kind of emotional floodgate opening, she felt the heat build up into an unexpected second release. When it exploded inside of her moments later and Aidan gave in to his own pleasure, she found herself on the verge of happy tears. She wanted to hold him, to hang on to this moment and cherish it forever.

A part of her wanted to tell him how she felt right then, but her logical side overrode it. It was one thing to fall in love quickly, another to announce it and have the timing be bad. Aidan might not be as in tune with his emotions. He might need more time to realize that what they had together was special and rare.

As he collapsed off to her side, the cool air danced across her damp, exposed skin, bringing a chill. She rolled against Aidan's side and snuggled into the nook of his arm. She felt safe and protected there, like everything outside of her apartment couldn't get to them. Things like her parents' disapproval.

Violet knew that was a discussion that needed to be had, and soon. But not tonight. Her parents were still in Eastern Europe somewhere and she wanted to enjoy this moment with Aidan. An unexpected sinking feeling in her stomach followed that thought, making her cling more tightly to him.

As though the moment wouldn't last much longer.

The following morning, Aidan went back to his apartment to get ready for work. He wasn't opening today, but he wanted to head out to his mom's house to grab something before his shift was supposed to start.

Last night with Violet had made him start thinking about things he hadn't really considered before. They hadn't been together as a couple long, but getting up in the morning to return to his place was a painful reminder that their cohabitation had been a temporary thing. With her kitchen fixed, Violet was back home. That meant everything he'd gotten used to so quickly was over. Yes, he had a standing Sunday afternoon date to see Knox, but there was nothing to say that he had a standing date with Violet.

Yes, he was happy to be Knox's father, and involved in his life, but he wanted more. As impractical as it might seem, he wanted them to be a real family. One that woke up together and shared breakfast before starting their day. One

that went on trips to the park and the ball field.
Who cheered together for Knox's T-ball team.
Who went on family vacations and took cheesy
photos together that they would frame and hang
on the wall of their home.

Walking up the front steps of his mother's
house was a cold reminder that they didn't share
a home. Not in the same way his parents did. Their
marriage had been anything but perfect, but his
mother had loved and cared for his father until the
end. They had built a home and family together
in a way that Aidan longed for.

But would Violet ever consider something like
that? A real family? A marriage? Marriage hadn't
even come up when he found out about the baby,
and for good reason. If she did agree to marry
him, it would be because she wanted to, not because she felt obligated to because of Knox and
the societal pressure to marry his father.

That was both encouraging and frightening because he didn't know which way it would go. He
wanted Violet to say yes. His feelings for her were
still new and uncertain in his mind, but his feelings about the three of them were clear. No matter what she might say, he felt compelled to give
it his best shot.

Inside the house, he stopped at the bottom
of the stairs. Aidan had avoided going upstairs.
More specifically, he'd avoided cleaning out his

mother's bedroom. Right after she'd succumbed to her pancreatic cancer, it had been too painful to go through her things and give them away. Really, there wasn't a rush. It hadn't mattered until now if they sat and collected dust or got boxed up.

But with the money from the foundation and the charity event coming up, his administrator and first round of tenants would soon be moving in and Molly's House would become a reality. That would require a good bit of work on Aidan's part.

Most of the clothes and miscellaneous items would be donated to a shelter or charity. Probably to St. Vincent de Paul. The furniture that was good enough to stay would be used for the new residents along with items for the kitchen. Most of the people who would be moving in wouldn't have anything but a bag of personal effects for the temporary stay.

Anything that fell in the bucket of a family heirloom would go to his apartment. There wasn't much, but he knew there were a few things his mother took special care of. Knox would inherit plenty from his mother's family he was sure, but Aidan wanted him to have some things from his side, too. It would be hard to compete with a couple million or so dollars in a trust fund, but a silver pocket watch that belonged to Knox's great grandfather might be a special keepsake for him to have one day.

He forced himself up the stairs to the bedroom his parents had shared for his entire life. Everything was just as he remembered it, only covered in a light layer of dust and neglect. The room still held the faint scent of his mother's favorite rose perfume. Just catching a whiff of it in the department store was enough to bring tears to his eyes. Here was no different.

Looking around, he realized there was a lot to go through, but today, there was only one thing he was concerned about finding—one thing he didn't dare lose in the shuffle.

He strode across the room to the old oak dresser and the jewelry box standing on top of it. In it, he knew he would find his grandfather's watch, his mother's good pearls, a medal he'd earned in Boy Scouts and a couple other little pieces she'd cherished over the years. That included her engagement ring.

Aidan hadn't wanted to take it from her. He was just as happy to bury her with her jewelry, but she had insisted on it. Her wedding ring was enough, but the engagement ring was special. It had belonged to his great-grandmother on his father's side and was given to his dad when he wanted to propose. It was family and history and she'd wanted Aidan to give it to his future bride, not to let it rot with her corpse under the earth.

He'd finally relented, bringing it upstairs and

putting it in her jewelry box for safekeeping. He'd still held on to the hope that she would recover, come home and want to put her ring back on. That, of course, hadn't happened. So the ring had sat there with everything else over the last year.

He found the old satin-covered box just as he'd left it. It was the original container, worn and fragile, easily eighty years old. As he opened the tarnished hinge, his gaze fell upon the familiar ring he'd seen on his mother's finger nearly every day of her life.

Aidan didn't know much about rings or diamonds, but his mother had told him it was an art deco ballerina-style setting. He supposed that was a fancy way of saying it was a center stone surrounded by smaller diamonds radiating out around it like a sun or a ballerina and her tutu. All he knew was that it was beautiful and his mother had cherished it.

If it hadn't been an heirloom, he doubted his father would've ever been able to afford a ring like this. Aidan probably couldn't afford to buy one in this style, either. He couldn't stroll into Tiffany & Co. and drop six figures on an engagement ring like Violet probably expected to receive one day. Like Beau had probably already given her last year. But he could offer her this.

If she'd accept it.

He wasn't certain how she felt about him. Or

even how he felt about her. But he knew he wanted
to be around her and Knox every day of the year.
Not just Sunday afternoons and alternating holi-
days. He wanted to wake up to Violet in his bed
and he felt like if he didn't step up now he would
miss his chance. Violet was easily one of the most
eligible women in Manhattan. Even if Beau was
out of the picture, and it didn't seem like he was
ready to go quietly, someone else might come
along.

If he wanted Violet, he needed to let her know
before she found someone who would fit more
easily into her life and her family.

The idea of someone else taking his place made
his blood boil. He wasn't that great with feelings,
but he knew that meant something. And if that
something meant he needed to ask her to marry
him, then he would ask her to marry him and
hope for the best.

Holding the ring up to the light, he twirled it
between his fingertips to watch the colors dance.
It would look beautiful on Violet's hand.

Taking a deep breath, he put the ring back in
its box and headed downstairs. Soon, he told himself. Soon.

Ten

"The turnout for the event is amazing."

Violet stood at the edge of the ballroom with her assistant, Betsy, as they admired the crowd. She was right. Betsy had worked for the Niarchos Foundation long before Violet was in charge and knew a successful event when she saw one. They'd had one of their highest RSVPs ever for the charity gala and she was pleased to know it was all going to benefit Aidan and Molly's House. The band was great, the dance floor was filled with people, and more in their finery and masks were showing up every second.

"I do have a question for you, though," Betsy added.

"What's that?" Violet eyed the crowd, looking for Aidan, but she hadn't spotted him yet. She was anxious to see him in his new tuxedo. He looked damn sexy in his snug jeans and tight-fitting T-shirts, but there was something about a man in a great tux that brought all her James Bond fantasies to life.

"Your parents. I noticed they aren't on the guest list for tonight."

She pulled her attention back to her assistant, curious as to her line of questioning. "And?"

"And," Betsy said, "this is their foundation. We usually invite them to all the events."

"I think they're in Romania," Violet said dismissively. "What's the point in sending them an invitation when it's just going to stack up with the rest of their mail? We're trying to raise money, not spend it unnecessarily."

Betsy was a woman in her late fifties who rarely took nonsense from anyone. As she looked over her tortoiseshell glasses at Violet, her pointed expression made Violet think that perhaps she'd protested too much. Yes, they typically invited her parents. But typically, her lover and father of her child was not also at the event. There was no way they could look at Aidan and Violet together and not at least suspect that he was Knox's father. Even with a mask on, his hair would give him away.

That would open up a can of worms best left sealed for now. She hadn't told them about Aidan yet and she wasn't ready to. He had enough on his plate at the moment without being subjected to the scrutiny of the lovely Mr. and Mrs. Niarchos. They certainly didn't need the truth blowing up at a black-tie fundraiser with every important person in Manhattan watching with interest lighting their bloodthirsty gazes.

"Well, I hope you're telling me the truth, because your parents got home from Romania yesterday afternoon."

Violet stiffened and began nervously fidgeting with her Cartier diamond bracelet. "Oh, did they? They're not that great at keeping me up to date with their itineraries."

"Yes, your father came into the foundation yesterday after you'd left for the day. When I mentioned the gala, he seemed surprised to hear about it and that's when I realized they weren't on the guest list."

There was no suppressing Violet's expression of wide-eyed horror as she turned back to Betsy. "Betsy, is Father coming tonight?"

Betsy bit at her lip as though she were hesitant to say the words aloud. "He is. Both he and your mother are planning to come. But I didn't know you didn't want him here or I wouldn't have said anything to him. I thought it was just an oversight. There's nothing I can do about it now."

"It's not that I didn't want them to come," Violet said, hoping her shocked reaction wouldn't get back to her parents somehow. "I'm just avoiding having an important conversation with them and I don't want to do it here, tonight."

"About Mr. Rosso?"

Violet blinked a few times in confusion. What did her ex-fiancé have to do with any of this? "What makes you think this has something to do with Beau?"

Now Betsy looked as though she wanted to disappear into the velvet drapes behind her. "Because they're bringing him with them tonight," she said in a voice so small, Violet almost didn't hear her.

"What?" Everyone nearby heard Violet's sharp response, with several people turning to look their way. "Are you serious? Beau will be here tonight, too?"

"I'm afraid so. You know how they are. Every time they come back into town, they ask me if Beau has come around the office or if you two have reconciled. With the champagne flowing and the slow dancing, they probably figured it would be a good environment for romance. They're so anxious to have you and Beau get back together."

"Yes, I'm aware of that." Violet turned back to

the crowd, this time her eyes seeking out not only Aidan, but her parents and ex-fiancé, as well. The bottom had fallen out of her stomach, making it ache with worry. She took a few sips of merlot to drown the sensation, but it didn't work.

"Have I screwed up, Miss Niarchos?"

"No, Betsy." Violet used her most calm and practiced voice. "You had no reason to think it was an issue. It's my fault for not telling you. I should've known this would happen anyway. It's my luck."

"Would it help at all if I were to say that you look lovely tonight?" Betsy offered. "The copper shade of your gown is stunning with your coloring."

"Thank you, Betsy," Violet said.

It had taken her hours to choose a dress for tonight. She wanted just the right thing so she would look amazing on Aidan's arm. In the end, she'd opted for a taupe halter gown that was covered on the top with copper metallic beading and sequins that faded away down the length, leaving only the draping, sheer fabric from the knee down. The dress had a cluster of copper flowers around her throat, so she'd worn her dark hair up in a messy chignon and opted for only a fancy bracelet and understated earrings to go with it.

She couldn't tell Betsy that she'd chosen the

color because it reminded her of Aidan's hair, though.

"Oh, look," Betsy said. "Here comes Mr. Murphy."

The couples scattered from the dance floor as a song ended, revealing Aidan as he strolled toward her. When his light blue gaze met hers, she forgot about all her other worries for tonight. He was always handsome with his strong build and wild ginger hair, but tonight with that tailored Tom Ford tux, she had to remind herself not to stare. Not even the black satin mask he was wearing could obscure how sexy he looked. In fact, it just highlighted his piercing eyes, square jaw and full mouth. She couldn't wait to feel that mouth on her body once again.

He approached with a coy smile that made her core melt and the collar of her gown feel uncomfortably tight. "Good evening, ladies."

"Good evening, Mr. Murphy," Betsy said in a chipper voice. "You're looking so handsome tonight."

Aidan turned to the assistant and took her hand in greeting. "Why thank you. You're looking lovely yourself. Perhaps you'll grant me the honor of a spin around the dance floor later." He lifted the back of her hand to his lips and kissed it.

Betsy blushed crimson from her cheeks to the respectable amount of cleavage her black beaded gown revealed. She quickly brought her mask up to her face to cover it, but it was too late. Violet had never seen Betsy react this way to anyone. It seemed that women of all ages were quick to succumb to Aidan's charms. Violet hadn't stood a chance, really. He was handsome, charming, thoughtful and the sexiest devil she'd ever had the pleasure of sharing a bed with.

No wonder she was in love with him.

"And you are looking stunning tonight, Miss Niarchos." Aidan turned his attention to Violet, taking her hand and kissing it, too.

The warm press of his lips on her skin sent a shiver up her arm and down her spine. The simple touch was enough to make her nipples tighten with anticipation and press eagerly against the silky fabric of her dress. She tried not to squirm, delicately extracting her hand before anyone nearby noticed how their touch lingered.

"And where, pray tell, is your mask? This is a masquerade party, isn't it?"

Violet sighed and reached into her small clutch to pull it out. It was a copper metallic mask, with intricate swirling cutouts. The color perfectly matched her dress, but she'd been too busy worrying about getting the party started to put it on. Pressing it to her face, she tied the satin ribbon behind her head. "Is that better?"

"In truth, not really. Now I can't see your beautiful face. I guess I'll have to settle for gazing into your enchanting eyes."

Violet giggled nervously, worried Betsy would read too much into their exchange. "You're laying it on thick tonight, Mr. Murphy. Perhaps you'd better use that charm on the potential donors instead of me. I've already given you money."

"Will you excuse me?" Betsy smiled and headed off to the other side of the ballroom where something needed her attention.

Violet gave a heavy sigh of relief once she was gone, although she feared it would be short-lived. "Do you want everyone to know we're together?" she asked.

"I'm being charming. That's what you told me to do. I can't help it if my words sound more sincere when I'm speaking to you. I mean every one. I also mean it when I say that I'd like the next dance with you."

Aidan held out his hand, and Violet knew she couldn't resist it. "Just one," she warned.

"One is all I need."

Aidan led Violet to the already crowded dance floor. He made his way through the couples to the center of the crowd and then turned to pull her into his arms.

She moved into him, gripping his hand and resting her other hand on his shoulder. Even then she was stiff in his arms. She seemed anxious, although he wasn't sure why. The event was going smoothly. Just like everything she did, it was perfect.

He wondered if there wasn't more to it, though. The ring in his coat pocket felt like a hundred-pound boulder pulling him down. It was a constant reminder of what he intended to do tonight, although at the moment, he was rethinking his plan. It felt like a proposal would just pile more stress upon Violet, who was already strung tight as a drum.

"Are you worried someone will see us dancing and think too much of it?"

"Yes and no," Violet admitted. "Just be careful tonight. Betsy just told me that my parents and Beau plan to attend despite me not inviting them."

Aidan's brow knit together beneath his mask. Just when he seemed to think he was making progress with her, she would say something that set them back. "Why didn't you invite them? Don't you usually include them in foundation events?"

"I do. And they attend when they're in town. But tonight was different. I didn't invite them because I didn't…" Her voice trailed off.

"You didn't want them to see us together." Aidan felt a bitter taste rise up in his throat. He knew then that the ring was staying in his pocket tonight, no matter what.

God forbid her rich, perfectionist parents find out she was slumming with someone like him. That had to be why she seemed so adamant about keeping the lid on their relationship. "After everything I told you about my breakup with Iris, I can't believe you're going to stand here and tell me you didn't invite them because I'm not good enough for them to see us together."

Violet's eyes widened, filling the large space cut out of her mask. "No. That is absolutely not why I did it. Don't put horrible words in my mouth like that."

"Then enlighten me," he demanded.

Violet sighed and looked around them at the nearby dancers for a moment. "This isn't about you, Aidan. You are amazing. You're a great father to Knox. I love every minute I spend with you. This is completely about them. I didn't want to subject you to them until it was absolutely necessary. I've told you how they are with me… I'm never good enough. I wanted to protect you from that. But know that no matter what they say or do, their opinions are their own, not mine."

"Okay. Then kiss me," he challenged.

Violet stiffened in his arms. "That isn't appropriate at a foundation event."

Aidan only shook his head. "Maybe not, but do it anyway. Thumb your nose at the people who say we're not a good match and show them all we're together."

She glanced around the room, anxiously looking for someone. He parents most likely.

"Come on." He captured her chin in his hand and gently turned her face toward his. "Kiss me, Violet. Forget about everything and everyone else and show me how you feel about me."

"Aidan…"

"If you can't do this right here, right now, we might as well stop seeing each other and just stick to coparenting Knox. I'm not going to spend our whole relationship as a dark secret you're afraid of people finding out about."

Violet's delicate brow creased in concern as she studied his face. "You're not my dark secret, Aidan."

"Then kiss me and prove it."

Violet sighed and placed a hand against his cheek. "If that's what it's going to take for you to believe me, then fine. Let the whole world see this."

She leaned into him, reaching up to press her lips to his. He met her halfway, scooping her into his arms and holding her close. Then their lips met, and the world seemed to fade away for a while. There was no crowd, no disapproving parents, not even an orchestra playing nearby. It was just him and her. He wished he could bottle how it felt in the moment so he could remember it when life seemed too complicated.

Or once she was gone from his life forever.

A loud "ahem" interrupted the moment.

Pulling apart, they turned to find an older, well-dressed couple standing beside them. It only took half a heartbeat for Aidan to realize that it was Violet's parents. The woman looked like a more mature version of Violet with more gray than brown in her hair and soft wrinkles creasing her eyes and mouth. She was wearing a sparkling gray gown and easily half a million dollars in diamonds and gray pearls. The man was shorter, rounder and mostly bald, but he had shrewd dark eyes just like his daughter. Neither of them looked happy to find their daughter on the dance floor kissing some stranger.

Violet moved even farther away from Aidan once she realized who had interrupted them. Aidan noticed the move, but now wasn't the time to mention it.

"Mother. Father. You're home early from your trip," she said with a forced smile as she untied her mask.

Aidan noticed there was no warmth between them. No kisses or hugs of greeting after all that time apart. Not even a handshake. Just a polite, verbal exchange. He couldn't imagine having that sterile of a relationship with his parents, even when his father was at the height of his drinking.

Mr. Niarchos didn't comment on his daughter's words, instead turning to Aidan and ignoring her entirely. He studied every inch of him, then sighed heavily as though he recognized the similarities between Aidan and Knox and was less than impressed with the man who must be his grandson's biological father.

"Our invitation got lost in the mail," Mr. Niarchos said with a dry tone that indicated he didn't believe that for a second. "I'm glad we were able to make it anyway, however. Wouldn't have wanted to miss this." He looked from Aidan to Violet with a displeased scowl distorting his face.

"Mother, Father, this is Aidan Murphy." Violet started the introductions with a hint of nerves in her voice. "He's the one starting the Molly's House transitional home in memory of his late parents."

Her mother smiled politely, but her father just continued to stare Aidan down.

"Can I have a moment alone with Mr. Murphy?" her father asked after an awkward silence.

"I'd rather you didn't," Violet said, but her father gave her a stern look that made her confidence shrivel right before Aidan's eyes.

"It's okay," Aidan interjected. He placed a comforting hand on her shoulder, stroking her skin to soothe her and keep him from punching the other man for talking to her that way. "I'll be right back."

He followed her father away from the dance floor to a corner of the room that was more private. Private enough to talk, but not so much that there wouldn't be witnesses if things went sideways.

"I've been watching you two together, son."

Aidan straightened his spine, ensuring he towered several inches over her father, who wasn't much taller than Violet. He might be a billionaire wearing more in gold and designer clothing than Aidan would make in a year, but Aidan wasn't about to be intimidated by him the way Violet was. He didn't have any power over him. "I'm not your son. My name is Aidan."

"You're right. And you never will be my son, you understand? You think I don't know who you are with that bright red hair? The moment I saw you two dancing I knew the truth. But it doesn't matter. You haven't landed your meal ticket."

"Anyone who sees Violet as nothing more than a meal ticket doesn't deserve her," Aidan worked up the courage to say, interrupting him. Violet was smart and strong and a wonderful mother. To reduce her to the balance of her bank accounts was offensive.

Mr. Niarchos scowled at him for a moment and

then pointed a stubby finger in his direction. "Her future is with Beau. Someone who understands her and her life, someone who's of the same class and background as her. I don't know you, Mr. Murphy. I don't know if you're a plumber or a taxi driver or what, but I know this—you're temporary in her life. You might be Knox's father, but that won't matter for long. Violet will come to her senses and you will be a footnote in the story of her life, I guarantee it."

Aidan tried to hold as stoic a face as he could while the older man spewed his hateful diatribe at him. He wanted to fight back, to argue the point with her father, but since a part of him agreed with every word he said, that made it hard. Since the moment he realized that his disappearing lover was billionaire socialite Violet Niarchos, he'd had those doubts running through his mind.

He wasn't after a sugar mama. Honestly, the money was more of a detriment to their relationship than a perk. He already knew he wasn't good enough for her, and he didn't want to deal with the kind of rich snobbery that followed people like Violet around. He would always be judged, always have noses turned up at him, always be accused of using Violet. He didn't need that. He'd had enough of that at the advertising firm where he was one of the few self-made successes among a bunch of spoiled elitist kids.

"You may be right, sir, but that's Violet's decision to make, not yours."

With every ounce of self-control he had, Aidan turned and walked away. There was nothing more to be said between them. Both had made it pretty clear where they stood. Now he had to go or he would say or do something he would regret. Like it or not, that was Knox's grandfather.

It might be his party, but Aidan had had enough for tonight. The rich would continue drinking and mingling without him, he was sure. He had just cleared the ballroom when he heard a woman's voice shouting his name in the hall. He stopped and turned to see Violet rushing after him.

"Aidan, wait!"

He held his ground until she caught up with him. "I'm going home, Violet."

"What did he say to you?" she asked with concern lining her face.

"Nothing I didn't already know."

"Please don't take it personally, Aidan. He wouldn't like any man that wasn't Beau. Father's got it in his head that Beau is the right match for me. And yes, it would be easier to date Beau, but—"

"Easier?" Aidan interrupted. "Is dating me such a hardship? Is slumming at ballgames and eating hot dogs with me so horrible that you'd rather be drinking champagne and eating caviar on a yacht with an ass like your ex?"

"No. Of course not. All I'm trying to say is that it would be easier for us if we were more alike."

"You mean if I was rich, too, so you didn't have to feel self-conscious about your money and the fact that I don't have any."

"No, Aidan. I mean everything. Culturally, religiously, family history… Beau and I come from very similar backgrounds so there's less friction with things like that. We grew up together and went to the same Greek Orthodox church. We just have a lot in common."

"So it's not that I'm poor, it's that I'm poor, Irish and Catholic? Iris didn't even stoop that low. She wasn't much of a shining example of womanhood, but at least she was honest about money being the most important thing to her."

Violet dropped her face into her hands. "You're obviously in a fighting mood and nothing I say is going to come out right in your mind. So go home if you want to. Just know that I don't want to be with Beau, Aidan. I want to be with you. Because I love you."

If Aidan had heard those words at any other moment, his heart might have leaped with joy. But not right now. It just seemed like a bandage over a wound that wasn't going to heal anytime soon.

He was a fool to keep beating his head against the wall where Violet was concerned.

"I'm sure you'll buy yourself something pretty and get over it," he said before turning and heading down the grand staircase to the exit of the hotel.

Eleven

Aidan found himself wandering through the streets of Manhattan, unwilling to go home, and unsure of where else to turn. Instead, he'd just walked block by block until his shiny black dress shoes started to rub a blister into his toes. Stopping at a corner light, he looked up and spied the neon sign of a bar he'd heard of, but never visited before.

Crossing the street, he went inside and found it dark and fairly quiet. It wasn't a rowdy sports bar with dozens of televisions blaring or one offering a live band making it too loud to think. It was more the kind of place people went to drown their sorrows and hide away from the world for a while. It was perfect.

The bartender was a balding man in his forties with a graying goatee and bushy matching eyebrows. He nodded in greeting to Aidan and went back to what he was doing. Aidan found a seat at the far end of the bar in a dark corner isolated from any of the other patrons. He climbed onto the bar stool, immediately tugged loose his bow tie and unbuttoned the collar of his dress shirt. That helped lessen the irritating feeling of a lump in his throat that he couldn't swallow.

Now that he was off his feet, he was happy, but sitting still left him alone with his thoughts in a way walking through the city hadn't. A shot or four of whisky would do the trick, he was pretty certain. That would've been his father's solution. It was easy to forget your troubles in a glass until one day your troubles were caused by the glass itself. Tonight wasn't the night for Aidan to start drinking.

"What can I get ya?" the bartender asked as he came up and placed a napkin in front of Aidan.

"Ginger ale," he answered before he could change his mind and get something stronger.

The bartender arched a curious brow at Aidan, but didn't say anything. He just turned and went about pouring a soda in a tall glass of ice. Deliv-

ering the drink, he said, "Holler if you need anything," and disappeared.

He was grateful to be left alone. Bartenders had
a reputation for being amateur therapists, even
Aidan, although his father had a knack for it that
he lacked. Most of the bartending community enjoyed that part of the job and sought out the cus-
tomers who looked like they needed to chat. He
probably could use someone to talk to tonight, but
he wasn't ready. Not yet.

Instead, he sipped his ginger ale and stared intently at the wood grain of the bar top. The longer
he sat, the heavier the engagement ring felt in his
coat pocket. Finally, he took the box out and set
it down next to his drink. Opening the hinge, he
lifted the ring and twirled it thoughtfully between
his fingers. Even in the dim light of the bar, the diamonds sparkled brilliantly. It was beautiful, just
like the woman he'd intended to give it to tonight.

He was a fool to have even thought that was
a good idea. Spending that week living together
had tricked him into believing they could pull a
relationship off in reality. And maybe they could.
But proposing to Violet? A gorgeous billionaire
who could have any man she wanted? Just because
she'd chosen Aidan for a one-night stand didn't
mean she would choose him for a husband. She
probably wouldn't have chosen him for her son's
father if that was a decision she'd gotten to make.

Hell, he should consider himself lucky that her parents showed up and everything went wrong before he worked up the nerve to ask. He'd probably still end up in this bar, miserable and alone, but at least he'd saved himself the embarrassment of her turning him down in front of everyone at the masquerade party.

Because she would've said no, right?

Of course she would've. What did he have to offer her? That day when they ran into Beau, she'd made a big deal about how there were more important things in a relationship than success and money. But did she really mean it? She said she loved him, too, and he didn't know if he could take her declaration for truth, either. She was desperate to keep him from walking out on her, nothing more. He couldn't imagine she could take her father's side and then say something like that and mean it.

Then again, if he had truly listened to what she said with his brain and not just his ears, maybe he would've interpreted things differently. The argument had played in his mind a dozen times like a looping viral video. He realized now that she'd never said he wasn't good enough or that she would choose Beau over him as her father wanted. Just that her father had a point about them being different and how it could make a relationship harder.

That was true. They were different in every way, not just where money was concerned. And yes, that meant they would face challenges as a couple. They would have to have discussions like what religion to raise Knox in or whether or not he went to a swanky private school. But he loved her. And he loved his son. He wanted them to be a real family. If she truly loved him the way she said she did, they could make their relationship work.

If he hadn't ruined it all by throwing her love in her face and stomping off.

"Normally, I try to mind my own business, but it's not very often that a guy in a tuxedo with a diamond ring and no girl wanders into a place like this. Especially one throwing back ginger ales like there's no tomorrow."

Aidan looked at the line of empty soda glasses in front of him and smiled at the bartender. "I'd have to ask, too," he admitted. "I run a bar, myself."

"What are you doing here, then?"

That was a good question. He'd considered going to Murphy's. He'd even walked past it at one point. "If I went into my own bar, I'd end up working on a rare night off. Tonight I have other things on my mind."

"Like woman troubles?"

"You could call it that." Aidan looked at the ring, and then slipped it back into the box. "Are you married?"

"I was."

"Divorced?"

The bartender shook his head. "I'm a widower."

Aidan straightened up in his seat, suddenly feeling guilty for moping around when others had bigger problems than he did. "I'm sorry."

"Don't worry about it. It's been ten years now. I wish I could say I've gotten over it, but that would be a lie. I'm just getting better at talking about it."

"Was she sick?" For some reason, talking about the bartender's problems was easier than worrying about his own at the moment.

"No. It was an accident. One moment we were arguing about something stupid, and the next, she was gone."

Aidan could see the lines of regret etched into the man's face. Even a decade later, losing his wife seemed to haunt him.

"We were always arguing about stupid stuff," the bartender continued. "Her parents never liked me, so they were always causing trouble in our relationship by putting her in the middle. She was constantly trying to keep the peace, but I didn't want peace, I wanted her to side with me. The stress would build up until we would just pick at each other over little things. It all seems silly now."

After the night he'd had, Aidan could understand the issues the bartender had with his in-laws. "Why didn't her parents like you?"

He shrugged. "Name a reason and you'd probably be right. They didn't like anything about me. I wasn't educated and I didn't have a career with a future. My family wasn't the greatest. I didn't kiss their rear ends whenever we were together. They never seemed to care how much we loved one another or how well I treated her. She was my world. But after all these years, I've finally realized that basically anything I did would be wrong because no one was good enough for their only daughter."

"I can understand how that is. My... Violet... is an only child. Her parents have very high expectations."

The bartender nodded. "In the end, none of that mattered, but I didn't know it. I could never see what was the most important—that she loved me. That should've been my sole focus. Not all that other stuff. Instead of arguing with her, I should've been holding her tight. I should've been appreciating every precious moment I had with her, because I didn't have that many left."

Aidan wasn't sure what to say, but he knew that the thought of losing Violet permanently made him ill. Or maybe it was the four ginger ales he'd gone through since he arrived. Either way his stomach ached as he thought about living his life without Violet in it. Raising Knox without her. He knew he never wanted to know what that would feel like.

And yet, he'd walked away from her tonight and threw her love back in her face like a fool. What had he been thinking?

"Listen, I don't know what's going on with you and your intended. But I know this much—when you find the person you love, and who loves you, you've got to hold on to it. It isn't every day that you meet the person that makes you feel complete. When they come along, you've got to focus on what's truly important because that other stuff is just noise. What her parents think, what society thinks…it doesn't matter. Unfortunately, most people don't realize that until they lose that person for good. I know I didn't. And I regret it every single day of my life."

Aidan already felt an unbearable amount of regret swirling in his gut. He couldn't stand the thought of living with a lifetime of second-guessing himself. Reaching into his wallet, he pulled out enough for the soda and a hefty tip. The guy had earned it tenfold. "Thanks for the advice. I really needed that pep talk."

"No problem. You don't want to be like me. You've still got the chance to make things right with Violet. Don't waste the opportunity you've been given."

Aidan slid off the bar stool with a new sense

of purpose moving his feet. He was going to get a cab back to his apartment and once he was there, he was going to figure out how to fix this mess.

He loved Violet. He just hoped she still felt the same way about him.

Violet looked at the paperwork on her desk but couldn't get her eyes to focus on it. It had been that way for the last week, since Aidan walked out of the masquerade ball. She wasn't able to erase the image of his face as he said his hateful words and walked away.

She'd deserved some of it, she was sure, but she never imagined he would throw her love in her face like that. Violet didn't agree with her father; she was just trying to explain where he was coming from. Opposites did attract but in the long run, they made for a challenging relationship. She and Aidan had little in common aside from their son. She wasn't holding that against him, it was just a fact.

It didn't make her love him any less. It meant that maybe it wasn't enough. Perhaps being co-parents and nothing more was the right answer for them.

She only wished she could convince her heart of that.

A tap at the door interrupted her thoughts. "Yes?"

Betsy opened the door with an apologetic look on her face. "I'm sorry to disturb you, Miss Niarchos, but Mr. Rosso is here to see you."

Her stomach sank in her belly. She'd hoped for half a moment that it was Aidan, not Beau, waiting to see her. "Tell him I'm busy. He'll have to call and get time on my schedule."

"I did, but he is quite insistent that he see you right now."

Violet sighed. Beau was like a stubborn ox. He wasn't going to leave the office until he got what he wanted. "Fine. But interrupt us in ten minutes with an urgent call."

Betsy nodded and a moment later, Beau strolled through the door. He looked just as cocky as ever in his pinstripe suit, slicked-back dark hair and knowing smile. He strolled arrogantly across the room to her desk with his hands buried in his pants pockets.

With every step closer he took, she found it harder to believe that she'd almost married Beau. Yes, her father was right when he said that things would be easier with Beau. At least on the surface. But at the moment, the idea of dating Beau again made her feel very unsettled.

"Violet, I'm disappointed," Beau said.

She arched her brow as she looked up at him from her office chair. "Dare I ask why?"

"No kiss? Not even a handshake?"

Violet put out her hand to shake it and he brought it up to his lips. She squirmed out of his grip and buried her hand beneath her desk. "What can I do for you, Beau? I'm very busy today."

Beau unbuttoned his coat and sat down in her guest chair. He sprawled out, making himself more comfortable there than he should. "Well, I missed out on seeing you at the gala the other night. I got hung up in traffic and by the time I arrived, your parents told me you'd already left."

"I wasn't in the partying mood." And that was true. After Aidan walked out, she couldn't bear to go back into the room and face her parents. She knew she would do or say something she would regret. She hadn't wanted to hurt Molly's House's chances by tainting the event with scandal, so she'd turned it over to Betsy and called it a night.

"So your parents said. They said you'd had a fuss with Knox's father and encouraged me to come see you."

"Why? So you could swoop in and save me?"

Beau just shrugged. "Maybe. I thought perhaps you'd had a taste of what was out there and you'd come to your senses about our engagement."

"'Come to my senses'?"

"Well, yeah. We're good together, Vi. Everyone seems to know it but you."

"I'm not so sure I agree with that sentiment." Beau was hardly a perfect boyfriend, something her parents never seemed to understand. Perhaps their own relationship was so flawed they didn't notice the difference.

Violet hadn't noticed the difference either until she'd spent the last few weeks with Aidan. It wasn't just that he was a good man and a great lover, but he was a great father. The kind of father Beau would never be. There were so many things that she and Knox would miss out on without Aidan in their life. Beau couldn't compete as a father. He wouldn't play sports with Knox or take him to Yankees games. He couldn't even pick up the baby without him howling.

"I don't think you're in a position to be so choosy, Violet."

"Choosy?"

"Yes. I'm being the bigger man here. Overlooking your infidelity and raising Knox as my own son is a big offering on my part. Not many men would be willing to do that. I'm willing to marry you, Violet. I'm willing to forgive your little dalliance and move our relationship forward."

Violet narrowed her gaze at Beau and suddenly, something about his words felt familiar. Little dalliance. *Dalliance.* That wasn't a common phrase and yet it seemed like she'd heard it recently.

Then, just as when Aidan had walked into her office that first day, a wave of missing memories rushed over her. All this time, she'd wondered

why she'd ended up in Murphy's Pub that night.
Going out alone looking for tequila and oblivion
was not her modus operandi. And yet she had.
When her memories had returned about her time
with Aidan, this was the one piece that had remained out of her reach.

She'd convinced herself that maybe they'd had
one of their usual fights. They argued more than
she was comfortable with, usually because Beau
was staying out late or doing things that led her
to believe he wasn't ready to settle down. If she
hadn't gotten pregnant, she never would've agreed
to marry him.

And if she had remembered what she knew
now, she would've punched him in the face instead.

"You bastard," she said in her coldest tone.

Beau's eyes widened in surprise. "Excuse me?"

"How could you let me go all those months
believing you, planning our wedding, when you
knew the truth?"

"The truth about what? That you were having
someone else's baby? I didn't know that. I thought
it was mine. How was I to know you'd banged
some bartender? I thought you were faithful."

She had to admit Beau was good. He was going
to stick with his lie because he thought she still
didn't remember. "I meant the truth about you
and me. Because I *was* faithful, Beau. When I

so-called 'banged' that bartender, we had broken up because I caught you in bed with that sneaky little cow Carmella Davis."

The previously suppressed image was suddenly incredibly clear in her mind. Her apartment. Her bed. Her boyfriend. Blonde and buxom Carmella completely naked and taking Beau for a ride… They'd fought, he'd argued it was just a *little dalliance*, nothing serious, and she ran out, wandering the streets distraught until she ended up in Murphy's Pub.

"I don't know what you're talking about, Violet."

She planted her hands on her desk and pushed herself up to glare at him from above. Her cheeks were flaming hot with anger. "When I lost my memory in the accident, it must've been a godsend for you. You'd lost your billion-dollar meal ticket through your own stupidity and got a reprieve because I forgot about the whole thing and you could just continue our relationship like nothing ever happened."

This time Beau had the good sense to keep his mouth shut.

"You rushed to my bedside at the hospital. Held my hand. And all the time, thanking your lucky stars I didn't remember what happened with you and Carmella. But the doctors said I would get my memory back eventually. Weren't you worried about that?"

"Not really." He shrugged arrogantly. "When you turned up pregnant, I figured it was mine and I was in the clear no matter what. If you hadn't insisted on getting your pre-baby body back before we got married, I would've had you locked down long before your memory returned. Then that little redheaded brat popped out of you and ruined all of my plans."

"That's it." She pointed one finger angrily toward the door. She was a patient person, but she was going to go full mama bear on his ass if he didn't leave soon. "Get out of my office."

"Violet—" he started to argue.

"No. End of discussion. I mean it, Beau. I want you out of my office and out of my life. For good. I don't ever want to see you here, at my apartment, or kissing up to my parents. I want you gone."

She held her arm stiff, pointing toward the door with a stern expression on her face until he relented. With a low growl of irritation, he pushed up from his chair and marched out without another word.

As the door to her office slammed shut, Violet breathed a sigh of relief. Beau was gone and even he wasn't stupid enough to come back and keep trying after this. It was over. Her parents would just have to learn to live with disappointment.

That was all she was to them anyway. The difference was that now, she no longer cared.

Violet was in love with Aidan and she wanted to be with him more than anything. She just had to convince him that she meant it.

Twelve

The front parlor of his mother's house felt empty without all the knickknacks and doilies to protect the furniture no one was ever allowed to use. Now the room housed a large thrift store desk, a bookshelf and a file cabinet. The space had been christened as an office for the administrator Aidan had hired to manage Molly's House. Ted was five years sober himself and had agreed to manage the house and its tenants for a small salary in addition to room and board at the house.

So far, Ted had been great. Not only would he be good as a mentor to the people staying here, but he previously worked in construction and was helping Aidan fix things around the house. There were so many little things that needed to be taken care of and Ted was tackling them as quickly as they were added to the list.

While Aidan had every intention of going to Violet and apologizing right after his conversation at the bar, things hadn't worked out that way. Monday morning when he'd gone to the foundation to try to talk to her, he found she wasn't in the office. Instead, he'd been greeted by Betsy, who'd been kind enough to act as though nothing had happened at the masquerade party. She'd happily handed him a flash drive with the database of gala attendees and a huge check with his cut of the proceeds from the successful event. Thankfully, the little scene they'd caused with Violet's parents hadn't hurt the charity's chances. He was grateful for that. Betsy had also promised to let Violet know he'd come by to see her and to call him when she had a chance to talk.

While he waited for her call, he'd been focused on getting the ball rolling with Molly's House. First, he'd put his assistant manager in charge of the bar and took off a week from Murphy's for the first time since his dad had died. Making the most of it, he had been at the house 24/7. He'd bought supplies and some basic furniture and linens for the bedrooms and baths, paid a cleaning crew to come in and brought Ted on board. They were close enough now to opening that Ted was reviewing applications for their first tenants from the nearby rehab center.

It had taken up more of his time than he'd expected, but he decided that a cooling-off period never hurt anyway. Tonight, when he got done here, he was going to Violet's to spend his previously scheduled time with Knox. Since she hadn't called, Aidan wasn't entirely sure how receptive she might be to his apology, but he figured that was as good a time as any to talk to her. Even if they didn't repair their relationship, they at least had to be cordial enough to manage caring for Knox together. Tara had taken to going out during his visits, so they'd have the evening to themselves to chat.

He just wished he wasn't so damn nervous about it.

"Hey, Aidan?"

He placed the plastic floor mat beneath the desk for the new office chair and looked over at his office administrator. "Yeah, Ted?"

"There's someone here to see you."

That was unusual, but okay. "Send them on back for me." Aidan rolled the chair up under the desk and straightened out some of the computer cords running to the power strip.

"Aidan?" a familiar woman's voice said.

Looking up, Aidan spied Violet unexpectedly

standing in the entryway. He straightened up from where he'd been crouching and dusted his hands off on his jeans. "Hey there. I, uh…wasn't expecting to see you here. I thought I was coming to your apartment tonight." It was a long trip out to the house, and she'd never even visited before. That made him instantly anxious when he coupled it with the lines of uncertainty on her face. "Is everything okay? Is Knox all right?"

"He's fine," Violet assured him. "I suppose I could've brought him here with me this afternoon, but Tara was about to give him his lunch and I didn't want to mess up his routine. He gets so crabby when he's hungry."

"He takes after me in that," he said with a smile he hoped would make him feel less awkward. It didn't. Aidan still didn't understand why she was here, if nothing was wrong with the baby. She could've texted or called about most things and saved herself the trip. What could she possibly have to say that needed to be done in person?

"Do we need to reschedule tonight?"

"No. Tonight is fine. I just…" She hesitated with her dark gaze dropping to the hardwood floors he and Ted had recently refinished. "I didn't want to wait to talk to you. I've already waited too long, but things got busy at the foundation this week."

Aidan frowned. He didn't like the way she said

that. It felt way too ominous for his taste. "Do you want some coffee or something?" he asked to prolong the discussion. "I've put in a Keurig for the kitchen. Recovering alcoholics drink a lot of coffee, I've been told."

"Um, sure." She followed him through the house to the kitchen. She waited silently while he made them both a cup of coffee, and then they sat down together at the old kitchen table.

"I've eaten thousands of bowls of cereal sitting at this table," he said, hoping he didn't sound like he was nervously rambling even though he was.

Violet chuckled, warming her hands on the mug of coffee and gathering her thoughts. "This is a great old house with a lot of important history for you. I think it's perfect for your vision for Molly's House. I don't know why I haven't been by to see it sooner. I can't wait to see how it all turns out for you."

"Is that why you came out today? To see the house?"

"No. I'd actually gone by Murphy's first thinking you would be there and the bartender told me you'd taken the week off to focus on the house, so I came here instead. I wanted to see you today so I could tell you that I'm sorry."

He almost didn't know what to say to that. He'd had every intention of apologizing to her, and yet she'd come all the way out to the Bronx to apologize to him. "What are you apologizing for? I don't understand."

She sighed and shook her head, her gaze never leaving her mug. "I'm sorry for not standing up to my father at the gala. I should've spoken to them ahead of time about finding Knox's father. Instead I just avoided the whole situation for as long as I could and ended up putting you in the crosshairs."

"You couldn't have anticipated how your father would react."

"He's really predictable, like a stubborn old mule. You were worried that I was ashamed of you that night, but that was never the case. I was worried about my father seeing us together and sticking his nose where it didn't belong. Of course, that's what he did. I never should've let him pull you aside to bully you because it wasn't his place to tell you anything. I should've protected you from him. And even if I couldn't stop him, I needed to stand up for myself and for our relationship and tell him once and for all to stay out of my love life. But I was a coward and I ended up hurting you instead. I managed to drive you away when all I wanted in the world was for you to stay."

Aidan was thrilled to hear her say those words, but he tried to keep his cool for now. She seemed to have a lot she wanted to say and he was going to let her get it all out. "It's been almost a week since the gala. What prompted this revelation?"

Violet looked up from her coffee. "Beau came by the foundation yesterday and I ended up getting the last piece of my lost memories back. All this time, I'd felt guilty for cheating on Beau. My parents kept insisting that he must really love me to overlook it and raise Knox as his son, but it never felt right. Now I know why. I'd come to Murphy's that night because I came home and found him in bed with someone else. I broke up with him and ran out. I didn't cheat on him. He cheated on me, then when I had the accident and forgot, he just continued on with our relationship as though nothing had happened."

"Wow," Aidan said aloud, although he wasn't entirely surprised. Beau had an underlying sleaziness that had bothered him the moment they met outside her building. "I'm sorry he hurt you, Violet. I wish you had told me exactly what happened that night at the bar, so I could've told you sooner. It would've still been a year too late, but you would've known before yesterday."

She smiled softly. "It's okay. The timing worked out. He was trying to talk me into giving us another shot—probably at my father's prompting—and the memories returning at that moment helped me put an end to it for good."

It was all an interesting story and he was happy

her memory had returned, but Aidan wasn't quite sure why she was telling him all of this. Beau being gone didn't necessarily clear the way for them to be together. He wasn't the only obstacle. "I'm glad for you," he said instead.

"That really isn't the most important part, though. While I was talking to Beau, listening to him tell me about how we needed to give it another try, even before my memory came back, I realized that I didn't want to give it another try with him. Despite everything that should make our relationship work, there were critical pieces missing. Pieces that only you have ever provided. You're Knox's father. Not just biologically, but you have taken on the role fully. You're involved with him now, even when he's tiny, so I know how wonderful you'll be with him when he's older. Beau would never be that for Knox. My son was always more of a…complication for Beau."

While he was pleased to hear he was meeting her expectations in the parent department, it wasn't what he wanted to hear right now. He wanted to know that she wanted him to be in her life for her sake, not just for Knox. "Is that it?" he asked.

"No. I'm just getting started. Of course I don't just want a father for Knox. I've realized that I want you, too. No, not even that. Of course I want you. That didn't come out right. I want to be with you, regardless of what anyone else says or thinks or wants for my life." Violet reached out and covered his hand with her own. "I love you, Aidan. And not because you're my son's father. I would want you in my life even if I hadn't gotten pregnant that first weekend."

Aidan was stunned speechless. He wasn't quite sure how to even respond to that. It was everything he'd hoped she'd say and yet the idea of it scared the crap out of him. Although he knew he had feelings for her, and she'd said she loved him, a part of him didn't truly believe it could be true. Could a woman like Violet ever truly love someone like him? He was afraid to believe her.

"What about the things you said at the party? About how different we are. How things would be easier with someone like Beau? Someone that shared your culture and background. Nothing has changed in that department."

"And I don't expect it to. Love isn't easy. I've realized that even with all those things going for Beau, loving him after everything we've been through would still be hard. It would be more work to forgive and trust him than any obstacle the two of us would ever face. It might be work for us to navigate, but it can also be fun and exciting for us to learn about each other. I don't want us to be alike. I just want us to be together. And happy. Do you think you could be happy with me? And with Knox? To have our own little family?"

Aidan felt his chest tighten at the mere thought of having a real family with Violet. Childhood memories of Christmas and Easter, first days of school and Friday night cheese pizza, all came back to him. Having all of that for Knox, and sharing it with Violet, was the most amazing thing he could think of to happen in his life.

There was just one thing left to do.

Aidan had been unnervingly quiet throughout their entire discussion. He asked a few questions, but for the most part, had sat with his coffee and listened quietly while she cut open her chest and laid her heart out on the table. She had come here knowing that he might not be receptive to what she had to say. She was prepared for that, and yet, had hoped desperately for him to leap out of his chair, scoop her into his arms, declare his love for her and kiss her senseless.

When Aidan finally did move, he stood up with a stoic look on his face. "Would you excuse me for a minute?"

She nodded and watched him disappear into the living room and go up the stairs. She wasn't sure what was upstairs that he had to go there right now, of all the times, but she did her best to sit patiently and not overreact.

Even then, she felt tears of disappointment start to well in her eyes. She asked him if he wanted to have a life with her, told him that she loved him, and he just got up from the table and walked away. That was not how she imagined this moment going.

But then Aidan returned a few minutes later with something small clutched in his fist. "I'm sorry about that. I had to go get something important. It couldn't wait."

Violet sniffed back her tears, hoping they were premature. "It's okay. Take all the time you need. I know I've dumped a lot on you at once."

He nodded. "I know. But it's okay. I've spent the last week going over the gala and really, every moment we've ever had together. I've been trying to figure out what I could say or what I could do to convince you to give us a chance. A real chance. If we're going to be a family, there can't be any more secrets. If you love me, you love me when your parents are around. You love me when we meet some of your fancy friends and have to tell them I run a bar for a living."

"I do," she said, pushing up from her chair. "I love you all the time, no matter what we're doing or who we're with. I always will. I sat my parents down and told them that last night."

"What did they say?"

Quite a bit, but she would spare Aidan the details. "My father threatened to cut me out of the will."

Aidan's eyes widened. "Oh, no."

Violet just shrugged. "That doesn't matter to me. All my money came from the trust fund my grandfather set up for me when I was born. I don't need my father's money. I think he was just blustering to get his way. He's got to get used to not having a say in my life any longer. I'm almost thirty. It's well past time."

Aidan smiled widely. "I'm glad you said that because there's something I want to give you. To tell you the truth, I had this with me the night of the gala, but I didn't feel like the time was right. And then…well… I thought it was better that I hadn't."

Violet's eyes zoomed in on the object in his hand. She knew exactly what that was now. It was a jewelry box. It was unmistakable. She felt her heart start to race in her chest. Could it really be what she thought it was? Would she be able to hide her disappointment if it were just a pretty necklace or a pair of earrings?

"The two of us are different, but I think it's a good thing. The only thing that's ever worried me was that we're never going to be financial equals. I would say that there are few men on the planet that ever could be. And since Mark Zuckerberg and Bill Gates are already taken, there's even fewer than that in the world to win your heart. It's not easy on a man's pride to be in that kind of a situation, but there's no way I can ever catch up to you, so I'll need to make peace with that. I didn't realize how much it bothered me until I realized that I loved you."

Violet held her breath. He'd never said those words out loud to her. She'd said it at the party and several times today and he hadn't yet responded in kind. A wave of relief washed over her. He loved her.

Even as that worry faded, a new kind of anxiety built inside of her. Was this really the moment she was waiting for? Despite being engaged to Beau, she'd never had the proposal moment most girls dream of. When she'd discovered she was pregnant, he'd said, *I guess we should get married, then*, and they'd gone to Tiffany & Co. to pick out a ring. Violet didn't expect perfectly timed fireworks and a gospel choir, but it was not exactly a romantic and heartfelt proposal, either.

"You may not know this about me, but in a lot of ways, I'm an old-fashioned kind of guy. I would've done the right thing and offered to marry you the moment I found out about Knox if I'd thought for a second you were interested in that. And later, when you and I got closer and I decided that I wanted us to be a real family, that I wanted us to get married because I loved you and wanted you in my life forever... I had new worries aside from whether or not you would say yes."

Aidan held up the box in his hand, which was still frustratingly closed. "It bothered me that I could never afford the kind of ring that other men might be able to offer you. Because you deserve it, Violet. You deserve the biggest, sparkliest diamond ring that Harry Winston could make. And I couldn't give you that."

She wanted to tell him that it didn't matter what kind of ring it was or if there even was a ring. It might be a status symbol to some women, but Violet wasn't like that. The ring Beau gave her was nice, but it was clunky and heavy on her hand. She would be relieved to have something that was simpler to wear and she hated that he was agonizing over a moment that should be special and simple in its own way. She wanted to shout out that she wanted to marry him before he even asked, but she held her tongue. She did want to marry him, but she wanted him to say what he needed to say.

"I realized that the best thing I could offer you, aside from my heart, my love and my devotion to you and our son, was something that was important and special to me. Sentimental value is priceless."

Aidan opened the box at last. Inside was a diamond ring just as she'd hoped, making her heart flutter with excitement. The round diamond was set in platinum with a sunburst of diamonds radiating from the center. It was art deco in style, probably from the 1930s, making her wonder where he'd found such a beautiful antique ring.

"This ring belonged to my mother, and my paternal great-grandmother before her. When my mother got sick, she insisted I keep the ring and just bury her with her wedding band. She told me that one day I would meet a woman special enough to wear it, and thankfully, she was right. You are special to me in so many different ways, Violet. You're smart and beautiful and an amazing mother. It makes my heart hurt to think of waking up every morning without you by my side."

Violet's heart was pounding so loudly in her chest she could barely hear what Aidan was saying. All she did know was that he hadn't yet asked the critical question she was desperate to say yes to. Even then, he stood with the ring in his hand, looking at her expectantly.

"And?" Violet asked.

Aidan looked at her with a confused arch of his brow. "And…?" Then his eyes widened in surprise. "Oh! I forgot the most important part, didn't I?" He dropped down to one knee on the worn linoleum floor of his mother's kitchen. "Violet Niarchos, I love you so much, it hurts to breathe when you're not near me. I know that I'm not perfect, and I never will be, but I'm willing to spend the rest of my life trying to be the kind of man you deserve. Will you do me the honor of being my wife?"

Finally.

"Yes!" Violet shouted.

Aidan's hands were shaking as he took the ring from its velvet bed and slipped it onto her finger. It fit beautifully, sparkling in the afternoon sunlight. It wasn't too bulky or too heavy. And knowing it was a family heirloom passed down made it all the more special. It was absolutely perfect.

He squeezed her hand and stood up, pulling her into an embrace. Violet wrapped her arms around his neck, tugging him tight against her. When his lips found hers, she drank in the taste of him, so thankful she had a second chance to kiss the man she thought she might've driven away forever. She never wanted to let go and now she knew she wouldn't have to. He was hers and she was his.

Forever.

* * * * *

COMING NEXT MONTH FROM

HARLEQUIN Desire

Available July 3, 2018

#2599 SECRET TWINS FOR THE TEXAN

Texas Cattleman's Club: The Impostor • by Karen Booth

Dani left town after the rancher broke her heart, but now she's back... with twin boys who look just like him! Given his secrets, he knows better than to fall in love, but their chemistry can't be denied. Will the truth destroy everything?

#2600 THE FORBIDDEN BROTHER

The McNeill Magnates • by Joanne Rock

Reclusive rancher Cody McNeill refuses to let photographer Jillian Ross onto his land, but then a chance encounter at a bar leads to an explosive night. Now he can't let her go—even after he learns that she meant to seduce his twin brother!

#2601 THE RANCHER'S HEIR

Billionaires and Babies • by Sara Orwig

Wealthy rancher Noah Grant has returned to Texas to fulfill a promise, but what he finds is the woman he once loved hiding the baby he's never known. Can he and Camilla overcome what tore them apart and find a way to forever?

#2602 HIS ENEMY'S DAUGHTER

First Family of Rodeo • by Sarah M. Anderson

Pete Wellington's father lost the family rodeo business in a poker game years ago. The owner's beautiful daughter, Chloe, holds the reins now, so it's time to go undercover and steal it back! But what happens if the sexy businesswoman steals his heart instead?

#2603 FRIENDSHIP ON FIRE

Love in Boston • by Joss Wood

Jules wrote off her former best friend when he left years ago. Now he's back...and demanding she pretend to be his fiancée to protect his business! She agrees to help, but that's only because she wants to take it from fake to forever...

#2604 ON TEMPORARY TERMS

Highland Heroes • by Janice Maynard

Lawyer Abby Hartman is falling hard for wealthy Scotsman Duncan Stewart, but when she learns his present is tied to a secret from her past, can she prove her innocence and convince him what they share is real?

*Reclusive rancher Cody McNeill refuses to let
photographer Jillian Ross onto his land, but then a
chance encounter at a bar leads to an explosive night.
Now he can't let her go—even after he learns that she
meant to seduce his twin brother!*

*Read on for a sneak peek of
THE FORBIDDEN BROTHER by Joanne Rock,
part of her McNEILL MAGNATES series!*

Cody McNeill knew—instantly—that the lovely redhead
seated in the booth across the way had mistaken him for
his twin.

His whole life, he'd witnessed women stare at Carson in
just that manner—like he was the answer to all their fantasies.
It was strange, really, since he and Carson were supposedly
identical. To people who knew them, they couldn't be more
different. Even strangers could usually tell at a glance that
Carson was the charmer and Cody was…not.

But somehow the redhead hadn't quite figured it out yet.

Between the dark mood hovering over Cody and the
realization that he wouldn't mind stealing away one of his
brother's admirers, he did something he hadn't done since
he was a schoolkid.

He pretended to be his twin.

"Would you like some tips on what's edible around
here?" He tested out the words with a smile.

"Edible?"

"On the menu," he clarified. "There are some good
options if you'd like input."

The way she blushed, he had to wonder what she'd thought he meant.

And damned if that intriguing notion didn't distract him from his dark mood.

"I, um…" She bit her lip uncertainly before seeming to collect her thoughts. "I'm not hungry, but thank you. I actually followed you in here to speak to you."

Ah, hell. He wasn't ready to end the game that had taken a turn for the interesting. But it was one thing to ride the wave of the woman's mistaken assumption. It was another to lie, and Cody's ethics weren't going to allow him to sink that low.

The smile his brother normally wore slid from Cody's face. Disappointment cooled the heat in his veins.

The music in the bar switched to a slow tempo that gave him an idea for putting off a conversation he didn't care to have.

"Are you sure you want to talk?" Shoving himself to his feet, he extended a hand to her. "We could dance instead."

He stared down into those green-gold eyes, willing her to say yes. But then, surprise of all surprises, the sweetest smile curved her lips, transforming her face from pretty to…

Wow.

"That sounds great," she agreed with a breathless laugh. "Thank you."

Sliding her cool fingers into his palm, she rose and let him lead her to the dance floor.

Don't miss
THE FORBIDDEN BROTHER by Joanne Rock,
part of her McNEILL MAGNATES series!

Available July 2018 wherever
Harlequin® Desire books and ebooks are sold.

www.Harlequin.com

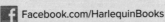
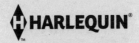

LOVE
Harlequin
romance?

Join our Harlequin community to share your thoughts and connect with other romance readers!

Be the first to find out about promotions, news, and exclusive content!

Sign up for the Harlequin e-newsletter and download a free book from any series at

www.TryHarlequin.com

CONNECT WITH US AT:

Harlequin.com/Community

 Facebook.com/HarlequinBooks

 Twitter.com/HarlequinBooks

 Instagram.com/HarlequinBooks

 Pinterest.com/HarlequinBooks

ReaderService.com

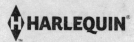

**ROMANCE WHEN
YOU NEED IT**

HSOCIAL2017

THE WORLD IS BETTER WITH

Romance

Harlequin has everything from contemporary, passionate and heartwarming to suspenseful and inspirational stories.

Whatever your mood, we have a romance just for you!

Connect with us to find your next great read, special offers and more.

f /HarlequinBooks

🐦 @HarlequinBooks

www.HarlequinBlog.com

www.Harlequin.com/Newsletters

◆ HARLEQUIN®

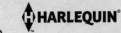

A *Romance* FOR EVERY MOOD™

www.Harlequin.com

Reward the book lover in you!

Earn points from all your Harlequin book purchases from wherever you shop.

Turn your points into *FREE BOOKS* of your choice

OR

EXCLUSIVE GIFTS from your favorite authors or series.

Join for FREE today at
www.HarlequinMyRewards.com.

Harlequin My Rewards is a free program (no fees) without any commitments or obligations.